The Space Program

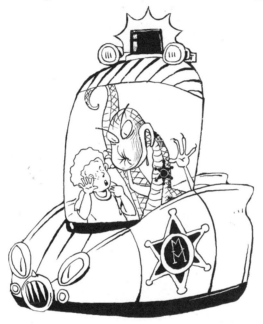

BY

JOANNA METZGER

ILLUSTRATIONS BY

MARCELO ELIZALDE

MW00910092

To Mummy, who always reads my stories
—J.M.

To my mother, the oldest girl on Earth
—M.E.

Text copyright © 2007 by Joanna Metzger
Illustrations copyright © 2006 by Marcelo Elizalde
under exclusive license to MONDO Publishing

No part of this publication may be reproduced, except in the case of quotation for articles or review,
or stored in any retrieval system, or transmitted in any form or by any means, electronic,
mechanical, photocopying, recording, or otherwise, without written permission from the publisher.

For information contact:
MONDO Publishing, 980 Avenue of the Americas, New York, NY 10018
Visit our website at http://www.mondopub.com
Printed in USA

07 08 09 10   5 4 3 2 1
ISBN 1-59336-695-7

Library of Congress Cataloging-in-Publication Data
Metzger, Joanna.

The Space Program / by Joanna Metzger ; illustrated by Marcelo Elizalde.
p. cm.
Summary: Selected for "The Space Program," ten-year-old Roger
Webb is whisked away to a planet intended as a model society,
where members of diverse alien cultures live together in harmony
and peace, but he unwittingly becomes a pawn in a plot to overthrow
the king.
ISBN 1-59336-695-7
[1. Extraterrestrial beings--Fiction. 2. Life on other
planets--Fiction.
3. Schools--Fiction. 4. Utopias--Fiction. 5. Science fiction.]
I. Elizalde, Marcelo, 1953-   , ill. II. Title.
PZ7.M5676Spa 2006
[Fic]--dc22

2005034181

Contents

Chapter One

A LIGHT IN THE FOREST

O ne fateful August night, Roger Webb was out in his backyard, searching for a missing yellow-bellied marmot. He had been out there for quite some time—looking through bushes, behind trash cans, and in between woodpiles. Roger had raised and nurtured the animal all summer long, and he wasn't about to let three months of training go straight out the window… just like the marmot had.

A marmot is a creature much like a groundhog. It has a yellowish-brown color, long claws, and a grizzled tail. It makes chucking noises when alarmed and loves to burrow in the soil near rocks. That June Roger found the animal in the field behind his house and decided to use it for his Science Fair project at school. The entire summer, he had been teaching his new pet—whom he named Mr. Chuckles—to do certain things that most marmots cannot manage. He taught him how to juggle three marbles at once, whistle the song "Mary Had a Little Lamb," and stand on his hind legs while dancing the tango with a rag doll. Until that night, Roger was brimming with confidence that he would win first place in the Science Fair with his dancing, juggling, and musically inclined mammalian marvel.

Earlier that evening, Roger's mother, who was feeling out of sorts, was in his bedroom looking for dirty laundry. Mrs. Webb had a lot on her mind, so when she came across a shaggy, brown towel lying on Roger's bed, she didn't think twice about picking it up and throwing it into her laundry bag. What she didn't expect, however, was for the towel to come squirming to life in her hands, kicking and biting with fierce resistance. With a terrified shriek, she did the first thing that comes to mind when dealing with an out-of-control bath towel. And so you see...this was exactly how the yellow-bellied marmot ended up out the window.

It was becoming quite clear to Roger, as he roamed the dark yard that night trying to signal his wayward prodigy, that perhaps he had trained his marmot a bit too well. The marmot had become too clever for his own good. Roger couldn't find him anywhere! Since the backyard was fenced in, there was no possible way for Mr. Chuckles to have escaped into the field or the forest beyond the field, unless he had stacked three blocks of firewood against the fence, climbed on top of them, and unlatched the gate with his paws...which was precisely what he had done.

Roger stood by the open gate and kicked the pile of firewood impatiently. Now what was he going to do? How would he ever find Mr. Chuckles, who was obviously feeling rejected as a result of his sudden ejection from the bedroom window?

As Roger was looking beyond the field into the forest and wondering how he would ever find his disgruntled marmot in all that darkness, something unusual caught his eye. It was a blinking red light, barely visible through the treetops. Although a bit apprehensive about venturing into the woods at night, Roger succumbed to curiosity. He took a deep breath and began walking toward the forest. But suddenly a high-pitched ZZZZZZZZIIINNG filled the air, and he watched in amazement as something round and silver shot up from the trees and vanished with a flash into the black sky. Roger stopped in his tracks and stared up at the swaying pines. He searched the sky frantically to catch another glimpse of the airborne object, but it was gone.

Roger's heart pounded as he continued through the field towards the forest—his eyes affixed to the sky, watching for further movement. He had always loved the sky at night. Looking up at it never failed to have a calming effect on him. The stars and the moon seemed so far away and mysterious, and they made him feel as if he were a small part of something much bigger.

The tall grass shifted gently in the breeze, and fireflies periodically lit up the sky like little sparks. When Roger reached the forest, he edged his way slowly through the dense branches and leafy foliage. The only things visible were the outlines of the trees and the twisted branches that surrounded him and cracked beneath his feet. A small, gray rabbit made him jump as it scurried past and blended into the leaves. Buzzing insects, croaking frogs, and the occasional hooting of a distant owl filled the air.

Ahead of Roger, it appeared as if something had carved out a large group of trees and left an empty, dirt-filled space in their absence. It was there that he noticed a metal box on the ground, partly concealed by leaves. It was small, blue, and engraved with odd symbols. He traced his fingers over the symbols and tried to open the box, but it was firmly locked.

Roger was confused. What could have happened here? He knew his account of events would seem highly unbelievable. But he knew what he saw was real. What Roger didn't know, however, was that before long, he would not only find the answers he was looking for, but he'd also discover that he was, indeed, a small part of something much, much bigger.

Chapter Two

THE STARGAZER

Roger Webb had just turned ten years old on July 17 and was about to enter fifth grade at McMurray Grade School. He had a full head of curly golden hair, blue eyes, and a charming, crooked smile. Roger was small for his age and somehow different from the other kids, which he didn't mind in the least.

Roger lived with his mother, Beatrice, in a little white house with a red tiled roof and green shutters. They lived on the far edge of a town called Pinewood, at the end of Shady Lane. Mrs. Webb worked at Stubby's Sugarworld Chocolate Farm in the center of town. The two of them didn't have much money, but somehow they were always able to get by.

Roger's father, George Webb, had disappeared when Roger was only four years old. He'd never said goodbye to his family, and he'd never returned. Roger only had a few memories of his father. He recalled going to the park on the weekends with him, feeding the ducks by the pond, and watching him point up towards the stars on warm summer nights. Roger also remembered being awakened late one night by his parents' loud voices and angry words. He had heard the front door slam, followed by footsteps on the driveway outside. Running over to the window, he'd watched his father get into his car and drive off down the street, the glow of the taillights fading away into the darkness.

The following day, three stern-looking men wearing blue FBI jackets came in and searched the house. Roger and his mother discovered that George Webb had stolen a large amount of money from his company and was wanted by the police. Instead of facing the consequences and accepting his punishment, he had simply left his family without any explanation.

His father's abrupt departure left Roger in a very bad state. He cried for months, and almost every night, he would go outside and wish on a star that his father would return. But return he did not, and all Roger had left to remember his father by was a small plastic crocodile that he had won for Roger at a carnival. When wound up, the crocodile was supposed to open its jaws, say "Yurrrr special," and then growl. But the battery had worn out years ago, and no one had bothered to replace it.

After her husband abandoned her, Beatrice Webb became sad and distracted. Roger's mother had always been a little eccentric, but as time went on, it was like she was walking around in a daze. Once she went to mail some letters and got halfway to the mailbox before realizing that she was carrying a frying pan—complete with first-class postage. On another occasion, she meant to answer the telephone and instead picked up the iron. (It was a very good thing the iron wasn't plugged in that day!)

Due to her distracted state, Beatrice Webb also had trouble keeping jobs, so she and Roger often had to move. This meant that almost every year, Roger had to start at a brand new school. At the last place they had lived, his mother had gotten fired from her job at the Waddington Zoo for accidentally locking the custodian in the primate cage overnight. The custodian had spent an entire terrifying night in the branches of a tree, singing soothing lullabies to a wild gorilla named Maggda. Needless to say, Roger's mother lost that job, and the two of them had to move again. So far his mother seemed to be doing well at the Chocolate Farm. Roger had been at McMurray Grade School in Pinewood for a full school year and was about to begin his second, a record for him.

"Hello, Mom," Roger said, as he came down to the kitchen on his first day of school.

"Oh...hello Roger," said his mother in the distant tone that Roger had grown accustomed to hearing. "Are you ready for school?"

"I guess so," he said. It was very difficult for Roger to hop from school to school every other year. He was missing out on the special bonds that form when children grow up together. As he got older, the difficulties of adapting to new schools got worse. He noticed that as the years went by the other kids became less likely to accept him. They viewed him as "the new kid" and not to be trusted. Their cliques had already been formed, and they didn't seem to have room for anyone new. This left Roger in a constant state of not knowing where he belonged.

"What's for breakfast?" Roger asked, sitting at the table.

"Uh...oh yes, breakfast," his mother sighed, shuffling towards the pantry. "I'm so forgetful these days, Roger." Her hair was disheveled, and her slippers had holes in them from years of wear. "How about some cereal?" She absentmindedly grabbed a box of rice from the pantry and plopped it down on the table.

"So, Mom," said Roger. "Last night while I was searching for Mr. Chuckles, I saw something kind of weird."

"Oh?"

"Yeah," he continued. "I saw something silver fly out of the forest."

"Was it an airplane?" his mother asked. She was kneeling in front of the refrigerator, rummaging through jars of food. Roger noticed a glass vase filled with pink carnations on the top shelf.

"Mom...the flowers. They don't belong in the fridge," Roger said. "And, no, it wasn't an airplane. It was way too low."

"Well," said his mother, taking the vase from the shelf and bringing it to the sink to fill with water. "It was probably a bird or a satellite then." She turned the water on, while clutching the vase.

"No," said Roger. "It wasn't that either. It was really fast. And there was a blinking red light on the top of it." He reached for his backpack. "I found something in the forest, too." He took out the blue box and held it out for his mother to see.

"Oh?" Mrs. Webb turned to look at the blue box. As she did, the vase slipped from her hand and crashed to the floor in a million shards of glass. The flowers lay in a tangled mess in a puddle near her feet.

"Those darn Martians are everywhere!" she exclaimed.

Roger, halfway to the broom closet, stopped dead in his tracks.

"What did you just say, Mom?"

"I said...those carnations were very rare!" She looked forlornly at the mangled flowers.

Roger stared at her. "Are you sure that's what you said, Mom?"

"Yes, I'm sure," she said.

"Because it sounded like you said..."

"Of course that's what I said. I bought those carnations from a man on the street who said they were one of a kind!"

Roger grabbed the broom from the closet and brought it to the sink, wondering how much money the man must have gotten from her with that lie. As he swept the bits of glass into the dustpan, his mother went over to the dishwasher.

"I did a load of laundry last night," she said, opening it up and taking out a pile of sudsy, dripping clothes. "Oh dear." Staring dis-

mally at the mess, she added, "I'm sorry, Roger."

"That's okay, Mom," Roger said, taking the soapy clothes from her. "I have other things I can wear."

"Your lunch is in the fridge," she said sleepily and walked zombie-like out of the room.

Lunch. That had always been a particularly disturbing time for Roger. Once he opened his lunchbox at school and found a peanut butter, egg, and pickle sandwich, with a side of ketchup and a bag of birdseed. His mother had mistaken peanut butter for mayonnaise and the birdseed for crackers. The other kids at the table pointed and *eewed*, but Roger just shrugged and ate the sandwich anyway. Another time his mother accidentally packed a sock in his lunch. Again everyone laughed—only that time, Roger didn't eat it.

□ □ □ □ □ □ □ □ □ □ □

Roger's first day of fifth grade went from bad to worse. After missing the bus, he arrived late to homeroom, where he was yelled at by his teacher, and then laughed at by the entire class for wearing two different shoes. (His mother had mistakenly cooked the others in a casserole the night before.) During art class, Roger spilled glue on his chair and accidentally sat in it, eliciting howls from his classmates and taunts of "Nice going, Nerdlinger." After another embarrassing lunchtime discovery (a liverwurst and jelly sandwich with a bag of buttons and a can of hairspray)—as well as realizing that he had a chunk of chewing gum entangled in his hair—Roger was ready to quit school.

As he made his way from lunch to the gym, he came to the bulletin board in the main hallway. It was packed with fliers, announcements, and sign-up sheets. Roger stood in front of it, looking dismally at the choices. There was a sheet for the music club, the soccer team, fall play tryouts, the math club, cheerleading, football, and the debate team. None of these things interested him. He was about to walk away when he noticed the corner of a bright yellow piece of paper poking out from behind the others. He pushed aside the layers of flyers to view it. Across the top of the sheet, in black letters, were the words,

THE SPACE PROGRAM. Sign up today.

The Space Program? Roger wondered. *What on Earth could that be about?* He figured that maybe it would be a club that met to look up at the stars or learn about the planets. Watching the sky had always been one of Roger's favorite things to do. Reaching into his book bag, he dug out a pencil. He scribbled his name on the first line and then placed the stack of papers back over the yellow one.

Roger headed towards his next class, feeling good that he had signed up for something. Now his grades would benefit from the bonus points that an after-school activity guaranteed, and with any luck, he might even make some friends.

Roger was so busy mulling over all the benefits of joining The Space Program that he didn't notice the odd, white-haired man with the crooked glasses who removed the yellow sheet from the bulletin board immediately after Roger signed his name and then lumbered out the front door.

Chapter Three

BROKEN PLANETS

E ach year at McMurray, students in grades 5–8 worked on a science project over the summer and presented it during the second week of school at the first open house. Teachers, parents, and other guests were all invited. Since the multi-talented Mr. Chuckles had disappeared (reappearing briefly one night to throw rocks at Roger's window before skittering off into the field with another marmot), Roger was forced to quickly come up with a different idea for his project. He had painted some Styrofoam balls to represent the nine planets of the solar system, stuck wire through them so they rotated when spun, and then attached them to a piece of black cardboard.

It was 6:00 P.M., and Roger's mother still had not returned home from work at Stubby's Sugarworld Chocolate Farm. The Science Fair was to begin in an hour, and Roger needed to get to the school to set up his table. He decided he would have to leave without her. Throwing a plastic bag over the display, he headed out the front door.

As he approached the school, Roger heard footsteps behind him. Turning, he saw Herbie Wergis and Bruiser Gunderson. They quickly caught up with him—circling him like a couple of sharks that hadn't eaten in days. Herbie Wergis was the most devious boy in Roger's grade. He was scrawny and weak, but his best friend was Bruiser Gunderson, the biggest and scariest boy in the school. Bruiser's real name was Buford Gunderson III, but he had earned the nickname Bruiser for obvious reasons. Roger thought Bruiser

Gunderson resembled an ape, both in size and intelligence. Herbie would pick fights with people for no reason and then let Bruiser finish them. The worst part about it was that Herbie Wergis had all the teachers fooled. They believed he was the sweetest boy who ever lived. He wore dress pants and ties to class every day, and he was known to bring the teachers apples and homemade cookies. Bruiser, on the other hand, had none of the teachers fooled. They all knew that he was a complete menace, but they didn't do much about it because, quite frankly, Bruiser was bigger than most of them.

"Hey, Roger. What'cha got in the bag?" Herbie asked derisively.

"Nothing—it's just my Science Fair project," Roger answered, without slowing down.

"Is it that whistling pig you've been bragging about all summer?"

"It's not...it wasn't a pig, Herbie. It was a yellow-bellied marmot, and no, this isn't the marmot," replied Roger wearily.

"Your goofy mom ran into my mom in the grocery store this summer and told her that you were raising some kind of pig." Herbie taunted. "Yeah, that same day my mother had to help your mother out of the pizza freezer. She'd gotten herself locked in there!" Herbie and Bruiser broke into a fit of laughter—guffawing and slapping their knees.

Roger felt the back of his neck turn red. He couldn't stand it when anyone made snide remarks about his mother. "I just told you, Herbie, it's not a pig," he said calmly.

"Can we see it?" Bruiser Gunderson said gruffly, stepping in front of Roger and forcing him to a stop with his big, meaty hands. He scowled and crossed his arms like a gorilla.

Herbie sidled up to Bruiser and glared at Roger with squinty eyes.

"I'm sure whatever it is, it's made out of Popsicle sticks and matches. That's probably all he can afford!" he sniveled, nudging Bruiser with his bony elbow.

Roger stared at the two of them, refusing to get upset. He had learned over the years that the thing bullies hated the most was when they couldn't intimidate someone.

"I'd rather be poor than stupid, Herbie," Roger replied calmly.

Herbie winced. The arrogant smile disappeared from his face, and he looked up at Bruiser, who seemed as if he were seconds away from growling and frothing at the mouth like a mad dog.

"Did you hear what he just said?" Herbie asked, his voice quivering with anger.

"I don't think I heard him right," Bruiser snarled, stepping closer to Roger and clenching his big fists. "Maybe he should say it again."

Roger was thinking *uh-oh* but was not about to let a scrawny liar and his ape-like friend bully him, no matter what the consequences. So taking a deep breath, Roger stared straight into the angry eyes of Bruiser Gunderson and responded, "Oh, I'm sorry, Bruiser, but I don't speak Chimpanzenese. Maybe that's why you didn't understand me."

Roger didn't have to wait long before he was thrown to the ground and had his Science Fair project ripped from his hands and smashed to pieces. He lay on the dirty sidewalk and watched as Herbie and Bruiser ran laughing towards school. He sat up and tried to straighten out his mangled solar system. Neptune and Mercury had come unglued. Mars and Pluto didn't rotate on the wires anymore, and a big chunk of Venus was gone. Roger sighed as he collected the sorry mess and headed to school.

Standing behind his project, Roger looked glumly around the gymnasium. He had straightened the planets out to the best of his ability, but compared to the other displays, his looked pathetic. He watched as everyone crowded around Herbie's Homemade Helper Robot, which was programmed to serve breakfast and coffee in the morning. He rolled his eyes as everyone *oohed* and *aahed* at the machine that had obviously been created by Herbie's father, who worked in electronics. Next to Herbie and his admiring fans was Suzie Green's multi-fruit tree, which had apples, oranges, grapes, and bananas growing from a single stalk. Across the room, Victor Chan was demonstrating his tornado in a jar. It looked as if a miniature tornado was whirling around in it. Victor had even put little bits of wood and small plastic cows in the jar to show the destruction a tornado causes. Down the way, Juan Fernandez's model of the city's water system, complete with working faucets and flowing rivers, was creating quite a stir. Roger sighed as his Saturn came unglued from the board and plopped to the floor with a weak thud.

□ □ □ □ □ □ □ □ □ □ □

The next week, Roger received an unusual phone call. It was a Tuesday night, and he and his mother had just sat down to spaghetti and meatballs when a shrill ring interrupted their silence. Neither Roger nor his mother were used to getting many calls, especially during dinner, so Roger was even more surprised when, after he said "Hello," a man with an urgent, nasally voice and a slight lisp replied, "Yeth, hello. Ith thith the rethidenthe of one Mr. Roger Webb?"

"Yes. This is Roger," he answered.

"Yeth. Hello. Of courthe it ith. May I athk the question, do you go to thkool at hmmm, let me thee here...McMurray Grade Thkool?"

"Uh, yes...I do. Who is this?" asked Roger.

"Yeth, uh, of *courthe* you do. Yeth. I am calling about the flyer that you filled out," the man lisped.

Roger thought for a second. "Oh, yeah! The flyer for The Space Program!" he said.

"Yeth, yeth. Of courthe The Thpace Program. Of courthe. Well, I am calling to tell you that our firtht meeting will be held eggthactly two moonth from thith moon, which is now half patht the thecond quarterly hemithphere of the galaggthic rotation of the planetary conthtellational gravitational thegment!" The man giggled nervously.

Roger held the phone away from his ear and stared at it in disbelief. He had no idea what the crazy-sounding man on the other end had just said. Had he said something about moons and quarterly hemispheres and galactic rotations? Roger almost hung up, but he was too curious to do it.

Putting the phone back to his ear, he said slowly, "I--I don't understand."

"Oh, yeth, yeth, of courthe," the man broke out into hysterical laughter, which sounded to Roger like a choking hyena. After the man had regained his composure, he said, "What I meant to thay ith that the firtht meeting for The Thpace Program (giggle, giggle) here at your thkool, ith going to be held two nighth from tonight."

Roger, again dumbfounded, said nothing.

"We can be eggthpecting you then?" the man lisped, hopefully.

"Uh...I don't know," said Roger reluctantly, having second thoughts about The Space Program upon hearing this bizarre man. "Who *is* this exactly?"

The man interrupted Roger frantically.

"Oh, no, no. You *mutht* come to the firtht meeting. You have been *chothen*!! I mean, you chothe uth, of courthe you chothe uth." Another outbreak of nervous giggles and choking noises filled Roger's ear. "But the point of all pointth ith that you thertainly mutht come to the firtht meeting." The man sounded insistent.

Roger thought it over for a moment and decided that all things aside, what he really wanted was to be able to join a club where he could look at the sky at night.

"Uh, okay. Yes, I'll be there. Where should I go?"

After Roger received the time and location of the first meeting, he hung up and returned to his spaghetti and meatballs, which were now cold.

"Who was that on the phone?" his mother asked, as she slowly twined noodles around her fork.

Roger thought for a second and realized he hadn't even gotten the man's name. He didn't want to tell his mother about The Space Program before he knew for certain that he was a member.

"I'm really not sure, Mom," he answered, which wasn't totally a lie.

"Oh." She shrugged and dipped a meatball into her milk. "That's very unusual."

Chapter Four

THE SPACE DIRECTOR

Two moons later, Roger waited until the sun had disappeared beyond the horizon and then stepped out his back door, armed with a big silver flashlight. He took a deep breath of cool night air and headed out to the large field behind his house, where the first meeting of The Space Program was to take place. Roger glanced at the skewed black shapes made by the trees in the forest, contrasting with the vast openness of the field. He had never liked the forest at night, but he liked it even less since the strange incident a few weeks back.

After walking for a while, he froze in his tracks when he caught sight of a still, dark figure sitting in a chair about ten yards away. Something seemed very odd about the way the person sat all alone and motionless in the dark. Roger slowly raised his flashlight towards the figure and saw that it was an old man sleeping in a lawn chair. The man was surprised by the light and held up his arm, shading his eyes and squinting to see who was there.

The man was someone Roger had never seen before. He had unruly white hair that sprouted from his head in every direction. He wore thick, black-rimmed glasses that were far too large for his face. The lenses were smudged and dirty, and one had a piece of tape covering a small crack. Roger also noticed that the man was missing four of his front teeth and wore disheveled clothing that didn't match. His pants were so short that his ankles were showing.

The man stood up to greet Roger, failing to remember a big stack of papers on his lap, which subsequently scattered in every direction.

"Ooh my, my, my!" the man said, in the same nasally voice that Roger recognized from the unusual phone call.

"Look what I've done now!! Oooh!" When he spoke, a faint whistling noise escaped through the gaps caused by his missing teeth. He tossed the papers in a sloppy heap back onto his chair, and turned to face Roger.

"Well, well. You mutht be Roger Webb," the man said with a broad, toothless smile.

"Uh...yes sir, I am," said Roger quietly, looking around nervously. "Am I the first one here?"

"Yeth, you are, you are," said the man, nodding vigorously. His white hair danced and his glasses slid further down his nose. "Pleathe thit down." He motioned to a second lawn chair.

Roger sat down cautiously. He watched the man stumble, remove the stack of papers, and sit down again. Missing the chair, he almost fell straight to the ground, righting himself at the last minute. The man burst out into another wild fit of choked laughter.

"Phew!" he gasped, pulling himself up. "That was a clothe one!"

Roger giggled quietly and then stopped himself. He didn't want to seem rude, but this man seemed like a bumbling fool!

"Tho," said the man, pushing his glasses up on his nose. "I would like to introduthe mythelf...and mythelf ith...I mean, I am...Dr. Ira Von Tibbetthon, director of the Thpace Program here on...I mean, here *in* your thkool here."

"Hello," said Roger.

"Tho..." continued Dr. Von Tibbetson. "It is my job as a Thpace Director to prepare you for your adventure. Firtht of all, on behalf of The Thpace Program, I would like to congratulate you, Mr. Roger Webb, for being thelected from the planet Earth to partithipate thith year. You...being in the fifth thector...I mean...in the fifth grade here on Earth...I mean...in your thkool here...on Earth...thith meanth that you are ready to begin your adventure."

Roger stared at the man in disbelief. In the distance he heard a dog howl.

"Sir?" Roger spoke up. "I'm not really sure what you're talking about. I think I may be in the wrong place. I signed up for The Space Program. You know, to look at stars and the sky and stuff. I think I'm going to go...." He started to get up, keeping his eye on the man and the big burlap bag on the ground next to him.

"Ooooohhhh!" exclaimed Dr. Von Tibbetson, clapping his hands together loudly. "How very thilly of me!!! Thit down, pleathe!

Roger slid uneasily back into his chair and watched Von Tibbetson shuffle the messy stack of papers around in his lap, mumbling to himself. Finally he reached into the bag and pulled out a book.

"Aha!" he exclaimed. "I've found it! You mutht read thith firtht. It'th probably better than my eggthplaining it to you ...(*chuckle, giggle*)...Thith will get you familiar with our little program here."

Dr. Von Tibbetson handed Roger a thick leather-bound book. On its cover, in sparkly gold letters, were the words THE SPACE PROGRAM. Roger ran his hand down the soft cover and slowly opened it.

Chapter One—The Space Program—founded in the Year of the Comet, Phase 4

Goals:

1) To promote friendship, tolerance, and acceptance throughout the universe

2) To enable diverse alien cultures to live together in harmony and peace

3) To establish a free and friendly exchange of trade among the galaxies

4) To make Mon-Marg the perfect society, a shining example for all others

"Mon-Marg?" Roger gasped.

"You, Mr. Roger Webb, are about to begin the adventure of a lifetime. You have a chanthe to do thomething that otherth on your planet will probably never get a chanthe to eggthperience. You can be a part of an ideal new world that otherth only dream about." Dr. Tibbetson's reassuring voice had a calming effect on Roger. The anxiety and fear that had previously gripped him slowly changed to curiosity.

"What exactly is Mon-Marg, Dr. Von Tibbetson?" Roger asked.

"Mon-Marg ith a planet that for many yearth wath believed to be a thtar. Yearth ago, the great thpace eggthplorer Sir Globbiouth Gloob from Blog dithcovered it wath a planet, and that it could thuthtain life! So hith idea wath to create a new home for the different thpecieth throughout the univerth. On Mon-Marg, everyone would live peathefully, free from hatred and violenthe. In order to make that pothible, he decided that he would perthonally dethide who wath welcome in thith new thothiety. Only the kindetht and most detherving from the univerthe would be allowed. It wath from thith idea that The Thpace Program wath born."

Roger looked up at the clear night sky and the silent stars that seemed to stretch for eternity across the vast blackness of the universe. They seemed to be winking at him, finally letting him in on their big secret. *There was life out there!*

"Where is Mon-Marg?" he asked.

Dr. Von Tibbetson pointed straight to the cluster of stars that formed Cassiopeia, the W-shaped constellation that had always been Roger's favorite.

"Do you see that thtar in the thenter?" He pointed to the center point of the W. "That is Mon-Marg. It ith eggthtremely far away.

From here it lookth like a thtar, so you can thee why Earthlingth might mithtake it for one."

"Wow!" Roger said. For all the years he had been looking at the stars, he must have seen that light a thousand times.

"Well then...well," Von Tibbetson was starting to get antsy. He started flipping through the disorganized stack of papers again. "I believe your take-off date is thkeduled for...let'th thee here...one week from today. Now before you go back home, I motht *definitely* need to give you a few nethethary thingth for thurvival on Mon-Marg."

"Wait a minute...who said I was going?" Roger asked.

Dr. Von Tibbetson smiled knowingly and began rummaging through the burlap bag. After an extended period of bumbling and mumbling, he finally resurfaced, holding gadgets in both hands.

"Now Roger, what we have here are thum objectth that you pothitively will need in order to thurvive on Mon-Marg."

Dr. Von Tibbetson gave Roger a silver utility belt with metal clasps. He also gave him a small box, which he explained was his "very own, thpecially-programmed *All-Alien-Language Decoder*. Thith allowth you to underthtand *any* alien language from *any* planet in the entire univerthe. You mutht be thure that it thtays on at all timeth and ith plugged into your Utility Belt. Every creature on Mon-Marg wearth one."

Next he held up an oval-shaped metal canister. "Now thith, Mr. Roger Webb, ith by far the most important devithe you will need on Mon-Marg. Thith ith what we call the *Aquarian-Andromeda-Atmothpheric-Pressure-Pack*. Or *Atmoth-Pack* for short. It hath the eggthact miggthture of the elementh that you will need to thurvive in the Mon-Margian atmothphere. All beingth on the planet have their

own unique blend, created ethpecially for their needth. However, the resultth of unplugging thith devithe would be equally dithathtrous for *all* thpecieth. You must *never, ever* unplug your *Atmoth-Pack* once you leave Earth." Dr. Von Tibbetson's face looked stern.

"What would happen to me if I were to unplug it?" asked Roger.

"Well," said the doctor. "You would have exactly ten minuteth for the reserve thupply to latht before you would thtart feeling breath-leth and notithe gravity decreathing. After thith, you would thlowly rithe off the thurface of the planet, float out of the Mon-Margian atmothphere, and thpend the remainder of your life drifting aimlethly through deep thpace. Tho you can thee why I streth that you *never, ever* unplug your *Atmoth-Pack*," he said.

"Well, I guarantee you, I will never, ever unplug my Atmos-Pack," chuckled Roger nervously, as visions of himself floating aimlessly through vast outer space flashed through his mind.

Finally Dr. Von Tibbetson gave Roger some *Read-All Contact Lenses* that would enable him to read all alien languages.

"OOOOOooooookay," said the little doctor when he was through. He gathered his papers and stuffed them back into the burlap bag. "My work here ith done. I think I have covered all of the bathicth. You are now thoroughly prepared for your take-off date on 20 October. I will thend a letter informing you of all the detailth."

Roger then watched as the strange man with untamed hair and missing teeth vanished into the edge of the black forest. He lifted his silver flashlight to try and catch sight of him, but the battery had worn out, and the light was a dull, fading orange. Roger stood alone in the darkness, listening to the steady humming of insects in the field, with only the soft light from the distant stars and moon to guide him home.

THE LOGGERHEAD SEA TURTLES

A few days later, Beatrice Webb received a letter explaining that her son, Roger, had been one of the few fortunate children from across the world to be chosen to attend the very prestigious Newton's Academy of Scientific Children. He would be offered the unique opportunity to spend the school year abroad—on a small island called Nahi-Nahi, off the coast of Australia—studying the relationship between the Giant Loggerhead Sea Turtles and the cycles of the moon. At first Beatrice was a bit confused by Roger's selection, seeing that his grades weren't all that impressive and that he had always been deathly afraid of turtles. But after countless hours on the phone with the President of Newton's Academy of Scientific Children, Dr. Ira Von Tibbetson, she was eventually convinced that Nahi-Nahi was the best place for Roger's "eggthepthional talentth."

On the night of his departure, Roger sat on his bed staring at the bags he had packed. They were stuffed with clothing, books, and the other necessities a young boy might need for life on another planet. In the side pocket, he had tucked away the wind-up crocodile that his father had given him and a framed picture of his mother. He also packed the other things Dr. Von Tibbetson had instructed him to bring—his Atmos-Pack, All-Alien-Language Decoder, and Utility Belt.

Roger still had trouble believing that he was actually going to live on another planet—one far away from Earth and everything that he was familiar with. He would miss his mother terribly, but knew she would be proud that her son had taken such a brave risk, even if she thought he was only going across the ocean instead of across the universe.

Taking a deep breath, Roger grabbed the heavy bags and trudged down the stairs to the living room where his mother was waiting. Mr. Chuckles, who had returned shortly after the Science Fair disaster (He had let himself in the front door and was in the midst of cooking a three-course breakfast when Roger had found him) was stretched out comfortably on the couch, watching the Wildlife Channel on TV.

"Are you ready to go, Roger?" his mother asked.

"I think so." Roger wanted to explain why he was going, but he wasn't quite sure himself. "I think I need to do this so I can find the things I've been missing, Mom."

"I am so proud of you," said his mother, as she got up from the couch and hugged him tightly. Roger felt tears well up in his eyes. "You're going to have a wonderful time and make lots of friends and learn amazing things at your new school. I think you'll find everything you've been looking for."

Roger wiped away a tear on his cheek with his sleeve.

"But I'll miss you, Mom," he sniffed.

"Well, I'll miss you, too. But you can call or write whenever you get a chance, and I'll do the same. After all, Australia isn't that far away, now is it? And besides, the Loggerhead Sea Turtles need you!" She ruffled his curly hair. Mr. Chuckles turned restlessly on the couch and scowled at the two of them, as he reached for the remote and turned up the volume.

A long silver bus pulled up to their little house at 3730 Shady Lane. Roger looked out the window and saw on the side of the bus, written in big red letters, the words Newton's Academy Charter Bus.

After hugging his mother one final time, Roger headed out into the dark night towards the bus. He looked up at the twinkling stars and felt a chill go up his spine.

"Here I come," he whispered to the stars.

As Roger approached the bus, he noticed that the letters on the side were peeling off. They actually read, "Norton's Arkademy Chatter Bug." Hoping his mother wouldn't notice the obvious spelling errors, he quickly climbed the stairs and saw Dr. Von Tibbetson in the driver's seat, wearing a uniform and hat.

"Good luck with the sea turtles, Roger!" his mother shouted.

Roger turned to wave once more. Then the doors closed behind him, and the bus pulled away. He stared out the window at his mother all the way down the block until they turned the corner and he lost sight of her.

"Well...hello, Roger Webb. Are you ready for your journey to begin?" Dr. Von Tibbetson asked, pulling the hat off his head. His hair was matted down, and Roger thought he looked like a sheepdog that had come too near an electrical socket.

"I think so," said Roger.

"Don't be nervouth...no, no, no. Mon-Marg is a wonderful plathe, you'll thsee," Von Tibbetson assured him.

"Will you be coming with me?" Roger asked.

"Oh, no. I have thum more work down here to do firtht. I will be theeing you later though," Von Tibbetson explained.

"But how will I get there? I don't know how to drive the space-ship! I don't even know the directions!" Roger panicked.

"Neither do I!" Von Tibbetson exclaimed. "Only the king himthelf knowth the thecretth to thspathe travel...everything ith taken care of ahead of time. Your entire trip hath already been programmed and the coordinateth plotted. You don't have to worry about a thing. You will be taken directly to Orientation Forest, located on the thurface of Planet Mon-Marg, where your very own Perthonal Greeter will be waiting for you," the doctor explained.

"Dr. Von Tibbetson?" asked Roger. "When I met you in the field that night, you said that I was selected to participate in The Space Program. What did you mean by *selected*? I was the one who filled out the flyer." It was a question that had been nagging Roger since he'd gotten the phone call over a month ago.

"Well," Von Tibbetson began. "Up on Mon-Marg, there ith what we call the Official Mon-Margian Thpace Committee, thelected by the king himthelf. The Thpace Committee hath a huge bowl that holdth the nameth of all the eligible children on all the planetth in the Program. Every year there ith a lottery where one name from each planet ith chothen. Onthe your name ith chothen, the Thpace Committee decideth whether or not you are the type of creature who would be good for our community on Mon-Marg. If you are a good candidate, they thend a Thpace Director—like me—to plant the flyer in your school. Nine out of ten timeth, the flyer is dithcovered and filled out." Von Tibbetson pushed up his crooked glasses. For some reason they were now missing a lens.

Soon Roger saw that they had traveled all the way to the edge of the forest and were at the exact place he had seen the silver object speed out of the trees weeks ago. Nestled among the dense trees was a shiny round spacecraft with a blinking red light on top. There were two circular windows on either side of it and a ramp leading to an open door.

"We have arrived at our dethtination, Roger. Thith ith where I musth bid you farewell and good luck." Dr. Von Tibbetson flashed a cheeky, toothless smile.

"Wow!" exclaimed Roger, in awe of the spacecraft. "I knew I wasn't seeing things! I saw one of these take off the night I was looking for Mr. Chuckles!" He left out the part about the blue box he had found. Roger didn't want Dr. Von Tibbetson to think of him as a thief. He planned to get rid of the box as soon as he got to Mon-Marg and had actually forgotten about it completely until that moment. He reached down and felt the secret pocket of his backpack. Sure enough he could feel the metal edge of the box through the nylon bag.

Von Tibbetson pointed to the spacecraft. "Thith here ith what we call your Tranthport Bubble. All you have to do is climb up the ramp, thit yourthelf down, thtrap yourthelf in, and wait. Make sure your *Language Decoder* and your *Atmoth-Pack* are plugged in. Your Perthonal Greeter will be waiting for you when you arrive. Any quethtionth?"

"I don't think so," said Roger, glancing nervously at the Transport Bubble.

"All right then. I wish you a mostht fantathtic journey. I'll thee you on Mon-Marg!"

◻ ◻ ◻ ◻ ◻ ◻ ◻ ◻ ◻ ◻ ◻

Inside the Transport Bubble, Roger sank nervously into a deep, plush chair. He reached around and buckled the seatbelt, securing himself tightly. As he leaned back and waited, his nervousness bloomed into full panic, which further multiplied when he saw the spastic blinking of a green light in the right corner of the craft.

"Here we go," Roger murmured. A knot formed in his stomach as he heard the soft purr of the engines starting up. Gripping the arms of the chair, he turned to look out the window at the smoky exhaust pouring out the sides.

Suddenly the Transport Bubble started to shake. The ship began sputtering and lurching slowly upwards, and Roger could soon see the roof of his house through the trees. But the rocking and teetering were the least of his problems. The control panels inside the Transport Bubble were making loud clanging noises, buzzers and alarms were screaming, and the small white lights that lined the ship were flickering. Roger became slightly dizzy.

The ship soon reached the tops of the pine trees, and Roger had an awful feeling that it might fall right out of the sky. As it lazily lurched higher and higher, Roger could see the entire field. He was just high enough to see the lights from all the houses down below.

ZZZIIIINGNGGGG!!!!!!!

Roger felt his whole body slam back into the soft cushion of the seat. He was hurtling upwards and thought his heart might drop right to his stomach. The lights from below had turned into specks resembling stars. The Transport Bubble was whizzing through the air with astounding speed. Roger watched as the individual houses turned into a sea of lights, outlining the entire northern hemisphere of planet Earth. He tried gasping for air and realized that he was going so fast he could barely breathe. He seemed to be suspended in space, careening towards his destination, unable to move from the force of the speed.

Soon Roger was far enough away to see planet Earth glowing blue and hazy against the blackness of outer space. It looked so peaceful tucked into its own little corner of the universe, and getting smaller as the ship sped deeper into the unknown. Roger thought it was the most beautiful sight he had ever seen. Then he lost sight of Earth completely, and a wave of loneliness swept over him.

The Bubble slowed down. Clusters of rocks and comets drifted past the windows, but none of them collided with the flawlessly programmed ship. The spacecraft passed Mars—glowing red, Jupiter's huge, glaring eye, and Saturn with its glorious rings. Roger stared in awe at the colossal planets before they disappeared, just as Earth had, into the darkness. The experience was like a glorious dream.

After traveling for what seemed to be an eternity but which on Roger's watch proved to be only ten minutes, the Transport Bubble began to descend. Roger stared out the window in amazement as a magnificent, bright pink planet came into view. A translucent, hazy glow surrounded it, and four thin yellow rings circled it like intersecting haloes.

"Mon-Marg!" Roger whispered.

AN UNEXPLAINED CHILL

The Transport Bubble landed smoothly on the surface of Mon-Marg. Roger sat very still and listened. All of the loud whizzing alarms and clanging had stopped, and the air around him was silent and motionless. He slowly loosened his rigid grip on the arms of the chair. It was now dark inside the spacecraft except for some dim emergency lights lining the floor. Looking out the window, he saw only thick, billowing exhaust steadily chugging from the engine.

Roger unbuckled the seatbelt and rose unsteadily to his feet. He had just flown through galaxies, passed stars and asteroids, and circled planets that he had spent his whole life studying from millions of miles away.

What will it be like out there? Who will I meet? Roger was so distracted that he almost missed the flashing red light in the corner of the Transport Bubble. He jumped backwards as the door began to inch slowly upward and a loud ticking echoed throughout the Bubble.

Tick…Tick…Tick….

Roger hastily grabbed his bags and scrambled towards the door. He reached down to his utility belt and made sure his Atmos-Pack and Language Decoder were secure. Standing near the door as the top of the ramp came into view, he closed his eyes. But as he stood there with his eyes shut tight, listening as the heavy door inched its way open, an unexplainable chill swept over him, giving him goose bumps and making the hairs on the back of his neck stand on end. It wasn't the type of chill he would experience if he were nervous, nor was it the way he'd feel if he were cold. This was entirely different. It was a feeling of pure and utter terror.

Roger didn't know why he felt this way, and he couldn't help but believe that the chill might be a bad premonition—that maybe he shouldn't have come to Mon-Marg at all. But before long the feeling passed, convincing him that it was just a case of nerves. Besides, there was no turning back now.

Tick...Tick...Tick....

Finally the door banged firmly in place overhead. Roger teetered on the edge of the ramp. The only thing that separated him from the new world was one small step. Taking a deep breath, he counted backwards. "Five...four...three...two...one..." Then he opened his eyes and stepped out.

□ □ □ □ □ □ □ □ □ □ □

Roger stepped off the ramp and bent down to pick up a handful of pink sandy soil. He watched it sift slowly through his fingers, glistening and sparkling as it fell into a soft pile. He looked around. The dark forest was engulfed in a thick fog, but he could still detect the distinctive shapes of trees. As his eyes adjusted to the blackness, he saw that the trees were lofty and straight, with smooth white bark. But the branches were bare and lifeless, and twisted in all directions, emitting strange, hollow clicks as they brushed against one another in the delicate breeze. The roots grew above the ground and gave Roger the impression of a frozen tangle of snakes.

Dr. Von Tibbetson had said that immediately upon arrival, Roger's very own Personal Greeter would meet him. But no one was there, so Roger sat down and waited on the ramp of his Transport Bubble, unsure of what to do. He leaned against his bags and kicked at the pink sand with the tip of his boot. He noticed that almost everything around him was perfectly silent and still. The only sound or movement came from the ghostly trees that clicked eerily like sticks of hollow bamboo.

Alone in the spooky forest, Roger was suddenly afraid. He couldn't escape the feeling that the looming trees were watching him, or that someone or something out there in the dark forest knew he was there...had been waiting for him. Shadows darted silently between the trees and disappeared into the sinister fog that seemed to swallow them whole. Roger hugged his backpack and almost convinced himself that it was just his imagination playing tricks on him. But then the howling started.

At first it was distant. Something far off was howling in a low, mournful way, like a lonely dog baying at the moon or someone crying out desperately to be saved. The miserable moan intensified as it crept through the air towards Roger, and soon the whole forest echoed with woeful howls.

Roger held his knees up to his chest and closed his eyes. He put his hands over his ears in an attempt to drown out the dreadful wailing. A lump began to build in his throat. Just as a warm tear rolled down his cheek, the sound of crackling branches arose from deep within the woods. The wretched howling diminished and then faded away.

Roger shuddered as he saw a shiny black vehicle emerge from the fog. It was low to the ground and had a glass dome on top with a tall antenna sticking up from the back. The vehicle itself didn't alarm him, but when the dome rolled up to reveal the driver, Roger jumped back several feet.

A small creature leapt out of the vehicle and landed unsteadily on two feet, regaining its balance with the help of a rickety wooden cane. The thing was no more than three feet tall and looked like a roly-poly ball of shaggy gray fur. It had an expressive face with two shiny little eyes and a black button nose.

Roger stared as the fur ball hobbled towards him, using the cane to move along faster. As it got closer, it straightened a black top hat trimmed with a glossy red ribbon. Then it felt for its Language Decoder and said in a flat and unenthusiastic voice: "Greetings. And welcome to Mon-Marg." The creature's little mouth twisted into a forced smile that revealed layers of surprisingly sharp teeth. "I am so sorry I'm late. I *do* hope you weren't waiting very long." Roger thought he detected a bit of sarcasm but he wasn't sure.

"Hi," said Roger.

"My name is Gwan," said the creature in a bored voice, as if his speech had been rehearsed many times. "And I am your Personal Greeter. I would like to officially say, Welcome to The Space Program!"

He lazily took off the hat, revealing two round ears and a single tuft of white fur sticking straight up from the top of his head like an arrow. He then took a deep bow in front of Roger.

"Thanks," Roger said. Then he remembered the howling. "Hey, did you hear those horrible moans just a minute ago? They stopped as soon as you got here."

"The Howling Whippterflash Trees?" answered Gwan. "Yes, if the trees don't recognize someone, they throw quite a tantrum. Once they saw me approaching though, they quieted down. Those trees really are hypersensitive whiners!"

Roger was relieved to know that he hadn't been imagining things. Something *had been* watching him while he waited.

"So, I suppose we should be moving along then. We haven't got all night." Gwan put his hat back on and twitched his nose. "Grab your bags and get in." He pointed to the vehicle that had been idling quietly between the trees.

"What is that exactly?" Roger asked as he collected his things and followed Gwan.

"Well," said Gwan, sighing, "this is an All-Purpose Vector. We call it a vector for short. It is the standard mode of transportation in and around the towns of Mon-Marg. Everyone 13 years of age or older can own one. You're not 13 yet, are you?"

Roger shook his head.

"No, of course you're not. I did my homework," Gwan said. "Not that anyone here notices," he grumbled softly.

"What was that?" Roger asked.

"Nothing," Gwan said. "Anyway, the All-Purpose Vector drives on land, flies through the air, and floats on water...but not in Lake Fuddle Mudd! You know to stay off Lake Fuddle Mudd, don't you?"

Roger looked at Gwan quizzically. "Uh...no, I'm not sure what you mean," he said sheepishly.

Gwan sighed impatiently. "Who is your Space Director? Let me guess, Von Tibbetson? Didn't he tell you anything about the Golden Rules of Mon-Marg?!"

"Not really."

"You mean he didn't warn you about staying away from Lake Fuddle Mudd or avoiding the Spitting Cactus Fields?" Gwan pressed.

"Uh...no...nothing like that...the spitting wha...?"

"Nothing about the invisible air shield to the volcano?" Gwan interrupted impatiently, "...or the Flintosorous cage...or the flying gypsy cats?"

"No," Roger sighed. "Nothing like that."

Gwan shook his head disgustedly. "How very, very typical. You aren't the first one of Von Tibbetson's assignments to be sent up uninformed. I really have no idea why King Gloob promoted him from Personal Greeter to Space Director. He is so muddle-headed!" he vented angrily, talking more to himself than to Roger. "Well, let's get going here. Hop in and I'll tell you about everything on the way into town." Gwan scurried over to the driver's side of the vector and threw himself in. "Hurry up!" he added irritably.

Soon they were rolling through Orientation Forest towards the town of Zirgon. Roger waited patiently for Gwan to explain the Golden Rules of Mon-Marg like he had promised. But instead, Gwan seemed perfectly content to complain about "that nitwit," Dr. Von Tibbetson, who according to Gwan was "an undeserving scatterbrain!"

"I mean, if he has the great honor of being a Space Director, the least he can do is learn his job and do thorough work!" Gwan slammed his paw on the dashboard. "He does this every time! He sends new assignments up without even teaching them the basics! Then I end up finishing his work for him and explaining everything, while he gets all the credit! And to think that I got passed over for promotion, and he got the job!"

Roger was beginning to wonder just *who* the hypersensitive whiner was in the forest that night! "Do you ever get lost in this forest, Gwan?" he asked, to change the subject.

"Well...not me," replied Gwan. "But once, about six years ago, a very experienced Personal Greeter went out to meet his assignment, just like I came to meet you tonight. He was going to meet an Inkytootian, the first of their kind on Mon-Marg. The Personal

Greeter must have gotten lost in the forest because neither of them ever made it back into town. Nobody knows what happened to them." He shook his head solemnly. "And we never went back to recruit any other Inkytootians."

Roger strained his eyes, trying to catch a glimpse of anything other than the trees and flickering shadows in the headlight. As he gazed at the fog-shrouded forest, the spooky sensation of dread passed over him again. It was the same eerie feeling that he was being watched, but something told Roger that it wasn't the trees this time. He quickly looked to his right and then to his left. As he looked at the path behind them, he caught sight of two shiny eyes and the silhouette of a figure crouching in the misty darkness. It remained there for a second before leaping off the path, disappearing between the trees. Roger swung around abruptly.

"What's the matter?" asked Gwan. "Is the forest getting to you?"

"I...I...just saw someone on the path behind us," stammered Roger, his voice shaking.

Gwan turned around and scanned the path. "Nope. There's nothing out there. I doubt anyone would be in the forest this late at night. It must be the forest playing tricks on you."

Roger didn't want to argue with Gwan, but he was certain that something had been out there.

"You know, being a Personal Greeter is really a very thankless job." Gwan changed the subject and began getting riled up again. "We are taken for granted. If it weren't for us, who would cart aliens like you through this miserable forest and show you around town? I take my job very seriously!"

Exhausted from his adventure, Roger tuned out Gwan's persistent complaining, closed his heavy eyelids, and drifted off to sleep.

Chapter Seven

ZIRGON

The vector lurched forward and then upwards into the air, waking Roger abruptly. It flew straight out over the trees, leaving the mysterious forest behind them. Roger gasped when he saw clusters of blue, pink, and white clouds swirling in misty patterns in the green morning sky. In the distance, a mountain range stretched clear across the horizon in a long craggy line. As they got closer, Roger saw that on the mountain tops, chiseled right from the stone, were castles with rocky turrets and elegant, stained-glass windows. Roger was amazed! These structures hadn't been built on top of the mountains—they were part of them!

"Those are the houses on the Top Tier, and the most lavish in all of Zirgon. Only Mon-Margians that hold highly important positions live up there—Space Directors, famous personalities, members of the Space Committee. Of course," he added bitterly, "I don't live on the Top Tier. I am just a poor little Personal Greeter. The work I do isn't important—even though I always end up doing the Space Director's job!" He shook his head angrily.

As Gwan continued to rant, Roger noticed to his horror that they were headed straight towards the mountain range. Just when Roger thought they were going to fly straight into the huge mass, Gwan slipped the vector through a narrow opening, and they drifted peacefully to safety.

"Welcome to Zirgon," Gwan said dully.

The town of Zirgon was surrounded on three sides by the mountain range. Hundreds of little cave-like houses were chiseled into the sides of the mountains in orderly rows, beginning at the base and continuing up to the Top Tier. Narrow, sandy paths wound around, connecting all the houses leading down to the town.

On the fourth side of Zirgon, a sparkling dark green lake bubbled gently, creating a fizzing sound as it churned and sputtered. Across the lake, far off in the distance, a majestic volcano rose up through the swirling clouds. A hazy glow shone from its peak, casting a blue tint on its surroundings. The volcano looked lofty and untouchable—and it was. Gwan explained that King Gloob lived in the volcano with his family, and that the shimmering green water was Lake Fuddle Mudd, which all creatures were forbidden to enter.

Finally Gwan brought the vector down to the ground on a small sandy path near the lake. "This is the city limit," he explained. "Vectors are not to be flown past this point—only outside the mountain ranges. We must now take to the ground and drive through town."

"Am I going to get to see inside the volcano, Gwan?" asked Roger excitedly, staring across the lake at the rocky dwelling. He had never imagined it was possible for someone to live in a volcano!

"Oh, no," Gwan answered, shaking his furry little head. "No one is allowed to go anywhere near it. If you tried reaching it by air, the invisible air shield would stop you. As soon as you got near, it would bounce you away...and not very gently, I might add. Even if you were to try to swim across Lake Fuddle Mudd—where you are not allowed to be—and try to find the underwater gate to the volcano, you would have no luck. The sand fog would confuse and disorient you. That, or you'd be stopped by the Muddshire Bogglings. But even if you got past them, you'd need the key to get inside the volcano gate, and nobody has that!"

"The Muddshire Bogglings?" Roger asked.

"Rumor has it there is a colony of sea rats guarding the gate," Gwan explained. "No one I know has ever seen them. Probably because no one is allowed to go into the lake! Here we are," Gwan said, changing the subject. "Are you ready?"

Roger nodded.

They reached the outskirts of town and turned slowly onto the central road leading into Zirgon. The first thing Roger noticed was all of the eccentric creatures milling about the streets. There were hordes of furry aliens, some with horns and scales, and metal robots with wings and webbed feet. He saw spongy, bird-like creatures with spiky tails and ten waving arms. There were walking insects, leafy lizards with big black eyes, and tall blue ones with only one eye and antlers. Roger gasped as a giant, coiled-up spring with eyes bounced down the street alongside a red balloon with a potato head and stumpy wooden legs.

They passed Zirgon Middle School, which Roger would soon be attending. Across from the school were the Personal Greeters' Headquarters, where Gwan both lived and worked. They traveled past a courthouse, a hospital, and a grocery store called Universal Food Emporium. Gwan also pointed out the Planetary Post Office—a busy-looking revolving glass building.

Gwan pulled the vector to the side of the road and gave Roger a few minutes to take in his new surroundings. Then they encountered a tall, thin creature wearing a police badge in the shape of a star. The lizardlike sheriff had scaly skin, glassy yellow eyes, and a sunken nose.

"Greetings, Sheriff Squarevicky!" Gwan called out.

"Well, hello there, Persssonal Greeter Gwan. Showing another

creature around town?" The sheriff's voice had a slight hiss, but his demeanor was friendly.

"Yes. This is Roger Webb from Planet Earth. Roger, this is our sheriff and one of the members of the Space Committee."

"Hello there, Roger Webb, and welcome!" The sheriff offered a black-gloved hand to Roger. "I'm Ssslee Sssquarevicky from the Planet Urg. I trussst you'll enjoy your ssstay. If there'sss anything you need, I'm right at the edge of town!" He smiled broadly and tipped his hat.

"Thanks, Sheriff Squarevicky!" Roger said.

"Take care now, you two!" The sheriff waved.

Leaving the sheriff, Gwan headed down to the end of the main road, which led out to the mountain homes. He pulled up to the base of the mountain, where Roger got out of the vehicle and grabbed his heavy bags.

"Here is the entrance to the housing section. You can only use these paths on foot. No vectors are allowed up there. Here is your home address." Gwan handed Roger a piece of paper. Then his voice took on the rehearsed tone again. "And remember, if you have any questions or problems regarding your stay or need someone to talk to, I am here for you. I am your Personal Greeter and friend. I can be reached at the Personal Greeters' Headquarters any time, day or night." He added grumpily, "Don't even try to talk to your Space Director, as he is always too busy flying around the universe, too busy to do what he is supposed to do and teach you about certain things that..." Gwan was clenching his fists now and shaking his little cane in anger. "And after I have been doing such a great job for so many years and then I get passed over for promotion, it's just not fair, and I..."

"Gwan!" shouted Roger.

Gwan looked up in surprise and composed himself. "Yes. Oh, yes. This is where I must say goodbye for now." He took off his top hat and bowed. "Welcome to Mon-Marg and good luck, Roger Webb." He gave Roger a big welcoming smile—the first real smile Roger had seen.

"Thanks, Gwan," said Roger. "I love it here already. I..." But Gwan was already turning the vector around. He sped away, blending back into the busy town.

Roger was alone. He saw no one as he climbed the winding paths up the mountainside. He kept walking past the little carved-out houses, all of them looking warm and cozy, glowing with light from inside.

It was now completely dark. Roger looked into the town from above, and paused to enjoy the gorgeous sight. The lights from stores and streetlamps lit up the town, and the buzz of activity could be felt from a distance. He looked further out and saw the blue glow of the glorious volcano. He noticed that it matched the blue moon far up in the night sky—a smooth, clear orb with no dents or craters on the surface. Roger also saw millions of stars shining down on him, and he suddenly realized that one of those bright, twinkling lights was Earth. The blue and green planet where he had once stood and looked up into the sky was now one of the millions of anonymous lights he saw when he looked at this new sky. *Fascinating.* He took a deep breath and continued his ascent. Somewhere up there, his new home awaited.

A FIRST FRIEND

Roger studied the quaint little house with the address Gwan had given him. It had a red wooden door and dainty boxes hanging from the windows, each filled with colorful, sweet-smelling flowers. Upon closer inspection, Roger noticed that all the flowers had tiny faces. Their little eyes were closed as they drooped in peaceful slumber.

Luminous candles shone from the windows, and an enticing aroma was drifting from inside the house—a sign that someone was cooking dinner. Roger was overjoyed, seeing that he hadn't eaten since he left Earth. He was a bit apprehensive of what to expect when the door opened, but he was too tired to wait. He knocked three times.

Inside, pots began clanging, cupboards shut, and then heavy footsteps were heard shuffling towards the door. Before he realized what was happening, a pair of long waggling arms embraced Roger tightly, lifting him clear off the ground. Another pair of arms seized the bags he was carrying, while still another pair held the door open.

"Well, hellllllloooooooo! You must be Roger!" A cheerful female voice bellowed.

"Yes, ma'am," mumbled Roger from beneath the creature's tight grip. His head was smashed against a fleshy stomach, which made it very difficult to answer—let alone breathe. Just when he thought he might pass out from lack of air, she released him. He straightened up and stood facing his new foster mother, struggling to catch his breath.

She was chalk-white and pudgy, with eight octopus-like arms. Her skin was soft and spongy like a marshmallow, and she had big emerald eyes that sparkled in the moonlight. Her long blond hair was human-like, pulled back into two braids that hung down past her chubby shoulders. She had a friendly, animated look, and when she smiled, her ivory cheeks flushed rosy red. Roger immediately felt welcome.

"My name is Mrs. Schleffinschlubb," she said. Her voice was high and lilting. "And it looks like you're going to be stuck with me for awhile! Come in! Come in!" She waved Roger in with her free arms.

Mrs. Schleffinschlubb waddled with big flipper feet pointed outwards, and Roger followed her down the hallway, which was lit by twinkling candles in bronze cups attached to the rocky walls. She lumbered along with his bags, swaying from side to side, softly humming a lively tune.

They reached the end of the hall and entered what appeared to be a kitchen, a small room also lit by candles. There was a table in one corner and something resembling a stove in another. Steel shelves—filled from top to bottom with bags, bottles, and boxes of things that Roger had never seen before—lined the entire room. A green powdery substance spilled from one of the boxes onto the floor. There were vials of bubbling liquids and bottles of smoking potions. He could have sworn that he saw one of the bags move.

Standing by the table was someone who Roger assumed to be Mr. Schleffinschlubb. He looked just like Mrs. Schleffinschlubb, only there wasn't a single hair on his round white head, and a long mustache drooped from under his plump nose.

"Most heartfelt greetings, Roger Webb," he roared in a deep voice, the hairs of his mustache billowing upwards as he spoke. "Welcome to our humble dwelling. Let me impart some knowledge to you regarding the dwellers of this domicile," he began in a scholarly tone. "We are Stanislavis and Stellvia Schleffinschlubb, and we are originally from Planet Scarfle, located in the Andromeda Galaxy. We are both employed at the Universal Food Emporium."

"Oooohh, which reminds me," Mrs. S. interrupted. "You must be starving!"

Roger felt his stomach rumble as she spoke. "Yes, I am," he said.

He got dizzy watching Mrs. Schleffinschlubb grab things from shelves with all eight arms at once, while at the same time walking, reading, and carrying on a conversation. One arm wrapped itself around a box of powder, another washed dishes, and still another was stirring a simmering cauldron on the stove. A fourth arm flipped through the pages of a blue book entitled *The Little Earth Handbook—Everything You Need to Know About Earthling Culture.*

"I've been studying this book, and I have been learning what your culture likes to eat. Although I must admit that some of the things made me queasy, I think I've found something that you'll enjoy here!" she said with a smile, blindly holding an arm out behind her. "Stanislavis, hand me that Fillywhipper..."

"I'm sure I'll love it, Mrs. S.," Roger said, feeling more at ease every minute.

"Why don't you ascend and acquaint yourself with Krin-Tin while we arrive at the denouement of hatching your dinner?" Mr. S. suggested, awkwardly dipping a puffy tentacle into one of the simmering brews and tasting it. "Krin-Tin just anchored from Orientation Forest this morning and has been upstairs slumbering the majority of the day. It is a conceivability that the two of you will have a gaggle of configurations to converse about!"

Mrs. Schleffinschlubb smiled apologetically. "He means to say that Krin-Tin just got here today and he's upstairs sleeping. You two probably have a lot to talk about!"

Roger was taken aback. "Who is Krin-Tin?"

"Why, Krin-Tin Nikkums is your roommate. Every year we take in two foster children," Mrs. S. smiled. "Go on, just walk straight out the kitchen door and then up the stairs. Your room is on the left. Put your bags down and make yourself at home."

"We will apprise the two of you when dinner is ripe!" boomed Mr. S.

Roger slowly opened the door at the top of the stairs. A flickering candle stood on the windowsill. In one corner of the dimly lit room, Roger could see a bunk bed and next to it, a pair of small white dressers. On the opposite side of the room were two desks and an open closet. Inside the closet, at least ten short-sleeved blue shirts hung side by side, meticulously spaced and perfectly pressed.

Glancing up at the top bunk, Roger saw the outline of a body curled up underneath a pile of blankets. He assumed that it was his new roommate. Not wanting to wake him, he quietly set his things down on the empty desk. As he did, Roger heard the pile of blankets turn restlessly. Then another strange sound made him jump.

"Hoooonnnnk"...and then a small pause..."Hoooooonk."

To Roger's surprise, the odd honking noise was coming from the pile of blankets.

"Hooooonk."

It sounded like an angry goose. And since he wasn't exactly sure just how to handle angry geese, Roger just stood there, weighing his options. He soon realized that the honking noise was consistent with the pile of blanket's breathing.

"Hooooonk" and then exhale. "Hoooonk" and then exhale.

Is it snoring? Roger couldn't believe that anyone could make such a ridiculous noise while sleeping!

"Hooooonk...Hooooonk"...and then, "Hick-hoooonk...Hick-hooonnnk..." Just like an angry choking goose!

Once the dreadful hick-honking began, Roger couldn't hold in his laughter any longer, and he broke into a fit of giggles.

The pile of blankets sat up with a start. Roger dove into the bottom bunk and put his hand over his mouth to keep from laughing. He leaned against the wall with his eyes wide open and his hand over his mouth, feeling a bit nervous about confronting the thing he had just woken with his rude eruption. For a moment, Roger could hear it moving around above him. Then there was silence. After what seemed like forever, Roger heard a small, shaky voice.

"Was my honking bothering you?"

Roger cleared his throat. "Um, no...I'm sorry for waking you. I, um..."

"That's all right. I've been sleeping all day. It's about time I woke up," squeaked the pile of blankets.

Roger leaned against the hard wall, wondering what to do next. After a long pause, he said, "My name is Roger Webb, and I just got to Mon-Marg tonight. I'm from the planet Earth, in the Milky Way Galaxy."

"My name is Krin-Tin Nikkums. I'm from Planet A-Zarg, in the Triangulum Galaxy. I just got here this morning," the blankets replied.

They sat in silence again for quite some time.

"How do you like it here so far?" Roger finally asked.

"I think it's a little strange. And I miss my family.

The Schleffinschlubbs are very nice though."

Roger paused and then said, "So, what was that honking noise, exactly?"

"It's just the noise I make when I sleep," said Krin-Tin. "I hope it won't bother you too much."

Again they were silent.

Finally Krin-Tin said what Roger was thinking. "Do you want to meet face to face...on the count of three?"

"Okay," said Roger. He was a little nervous to meet his roommate and hoped that Krin-Tin wasn't too weird looking.

"Okay then," said Krin-Tin. "One...two...three!"

Roger inched over to the edge of the bed and looked straight up into the big, blue, almond-shaped eyes of his new roommate, who was looking down into Roger's relatively small, round ones.

Krin-Tin Nikkums had smooth, green skin and a conehead with long pointy ears on either side. He had a tiny turned-up nose, and his mouth was small and round. He smiled when he saw Roger, revealing two rows of shiny teeth.

As the two of them stared at each other, Roger realized that he must look just as odd to Krin-Tin as Krin-Tin looked to him. Suddenly Krin-Tin swung around and dangled two scrawny legs over the side of the bed. He pulled on clunky boots, then jumped down and stood in front of Roger, who sat mesmerized on the bottom bunk.

The boy from A-Zarg was very skinny. He had long arms with four bony fingers on each hand. He wore an oversized blue shirt that came down to his knees, and his utility belt was loosely wrapped around his waist. Roger didn't quite know what to say next, so he blurted out the first thing that popped into his mind. "You look just like the aliens in the movies back on Earth!"

He immediately regretted it.

But to Roger's surprise, Krin-Tin erupted into a half-laughing, half-honking fit that caused him to start laughing also. Between hick-honk-laughs, Krin-Tin finally spit out the words: "I was…honk-haha…thinking …hick-honk-ha…the same thing about you!"

As the two sat and talked, they discovered many similarities. They were the same age and had entered The Space Program in much the same way. However, Roger couldn't help feeling different when Krin-Tin spoke of his loving family. He told Roger about his mother and father who loved him, and about his 47 brothers and sisters who were all going to miss him while he was away at Blogmott's Academy of Scientific Children, studying Flying Zibbergrottens.

"Will you miss your family?" asked Krin-Tin. His big blue eyes focused on Roger inquisitively.

"Well," Roger started to say, and then paused. He hadn't planned on telling anyone about his family on Earth, but Krin-Tin seemed very nice, and Roger felt that he could trust him with his sad history.

"I'll miss my mother, but I'm pretty sure that she'll be fine without me around. My father got in trouble with the police and left us when I was four." He pulled at a loose string from his blue jeans and tried hard not to cry.

Krin-Tin looked at Roger. "Well, you have a new family now—the Schleffinschlubbs and me! We're going to have a great time here on Mon-Marg. We'll go through the adventure together, and we'll stick by each other through rough times."

Roger felt tears of joy start to stream down his face as he promised to stick by his new roommate. Krin-Tin Nikkums from the planet A-Zarg—his first friend!

ANCIENT MON-MARGIAN HISTORY

Dinnertime! It is time to consume your nutritious repasts, young ones! An individual needs his vitamins in order to promote health and well-being!" Mr. Schleffinschlubb's thundering voice interrupted Roger and Krin-Tin.

The two hurried down the stairs, following the scent to the cozy kitchen where Mr. and Mrs. Schleffinschlubb were busy putting finishing touches on dinner. The boys watched as 16 arms moved simultaneously—grabbing spices, stirring soups, and folding napkins. Roger was becoming jittery just watching all the activity. Twice he had to duck to avoid being hit in the face with a plate.

"Sit down, you two!" cried Mrs. S. merrily as she scooped some runny gray mush from a boiling kettle and plunked it on a plate.

"Krin-Tin, you sit here." She pointed to the mush plate. Roger exhaled gratefully.

"Wow! Is this mushgruel? I love mushgruel!" said Krin-Tin enthusiastically. He unfolded his napkin and tucked it neatly into his shirt.

"Well, I was looking through my *Little A-Zargian Handbook*, and it says here that your planet loves mushgruel," she beamed, flipping through another small book. She tapped the spoon against his plate, causing the remainder of the gray slop to fall off in slimy chunks.

Roger scowled at Krin-Tin's food and slid apprehensively into the chair across the table. Suddenly a shrill clucking filled the room.

"Bruck-Bruck-Bruuuuuck!!" Mrs. S. pulled a small platter from the oven with a bird-like creature in the center. It had yellow feath-

ers, a pointy beak, and it was alive! Its round eyes were glazed over with fear, and the bright red plumage on top of its head swayed back and forth as Mrs. S. waddled to the table. The thing continued its shrieking until she set it in the middle of the table, where it looked from one chair to the next, blinking in confusion.

"Bruck-Bruck-Bruuuuck!" It flapped its little wings, unable to escape from the platter.

"What is that?" Roger asked cautiously.

"Well, you do eat chickens on Earth, don't you, Roger?" Mrs. S. seemed concerned. "This is a Goola Bird. *The Little Earth Handbook* told me to substitute one of these for chicken."

"But...it's still alive!" Roger exclaimed. The Goola Bird was now staring straight at Roger, with a frightened look in its eyes.

"Bruck-Bruck-Bruuuuck!" It seemed to be crying out to him.

"Oh, not for long." With a swift movement, Mrs. S. stretched one arm out to the cabinet and pulled out a long shiny knife. Another hand grabbed the bird by its feet, holding it in the air while it struggled and screeched.

"Wait!! Don't!!" screamed Roger, waving his hands frantically.

Mrs. S. stopped. "What's the matter? It tastes much better if the bird is fresh...it says so right here." She took another arm and desperately flipped through the pages of the *The Little Earth Handbook*. The Goola Bird dangled helplessly.

"Mrs. S., please...I don't want you to hurt that Goola Bird! Please! If it's all the same, I'll just eat some of Krin-Tin's mushgruel." He gulped with disgust at the sight of the gray slop.

"Well, if that's what you want, Roger. I just thought..." She put the knife down and reluctantly dropped the screaming bird.

"It was very nice of you to think of me, Mrs. S. I just think that it's going to take a while for me to get used to the different foods here on Mon-Marg." He sat back down unsteadily and watched as Mr. Schleffinschlubb spooned some runny mushgruel onto his plate. The Goola Bird, released from the platter, was shown the window. Roger wasn't sure, but he could have sworn that the bird smiled and winked at him before flying off into the night, reclaiming its freedom.

□ □ □ □ □ □ □ □ □ □ □

Roger pushed the putrid mushgruel around his plate while describing his adventurous trip to Mon-Marg, the Howling Whippterflash Trees, and Gwan's jealous outbursts. He was feeling quite comfortable in his new foster home. The Schleffinschlubbs were very friendly, and he and Krin-Tin seemed to get along well.

The Schleffinschlubbs were in the middle of telling a story about how surprised they were when they first arrived on Mon-Marg and discovered what electricity was, when Roger suddenly remembered something that he had been meaning to ask them all night.

"Will you tell us what happened in Orientation Forest a few years back?" Roger asked, the first chance he got.

The room suddenly became silent. Mr. Schleffinschlubb shot a nervous glance towards Mrs. Schleffinschlubb, and they both began fidgeting with things on the table.

"Why...whatever do you mean, Roger?" asked Mrs. S., clearly caught off guard by the question.

"You know, when the Personal Greeter and the Inkytootian disappeared," Roger said. Krin-Tin looked up from his plate in wonderment.

"Now what, pray tell, would cause you to ponder that incident?" asked Mr. S., clearing his throat and patting a napkin over his face. He glanced at Mrs. S., who suddenly pretended to be engrossed in one of her *Little Handbooks*, which, as Roger couldn't help but notice, was upside-down!

"While Gwan was driving me into town, he told me about the Personal Greeter and the Inkytootian who disappeared. I was just curious and wondered if you knew any more of the story," said Roger.

"Well," Mrs. S. took a deep breath, putting down her book hesitantly. "If you're really that curious...I'll tell you."

"Oh, we are!" Krin-Tin blurted out.

"Let me see then...it all started years ago, when King Gloob's trusted assistant, Bowgee Berg, discovered a new planet that had life on it. It was called Gorrinth and was located in the farthest corner of the Camelopardis Galaxy." Mrs. S. paused to take a drink of tree sap. Roger noticed that the cup clattered against the plate as she lowered it with shaking hands.

"Soon afterwards the king decided to invite five Gorrinthian children to be a part of The Space Program," she continued. "When the Gorrinthians—Gorrs, we called them—first arrived on Mon-Marg, everyone agreed that they were very nice creatures. After awhile, however, the Gorrs began behaving strangely. They began playing childish pranks, escaping from their homes at night, throwing things at windows...minor things. Nobody thought anything of it, other than that they were a bit mischievous."

"What did the Gorrs look like, Mrs. S?" Krin-Tin asked.

"They were scaly and white, with yellow eyes and sharp teeth. They sound terrifying, but I assure you that when they first arrived, they were angels," Mrs. S. answered.

"Anyway," she went on, "soon the Gorrs' behavior became more serious in nature. They set off the Spitting Cactus Trees and toyed with traffic lights, causing terrible vector accidents. They were even caught in Lake Fuddle Mudd! Not long after these events, the incident in Orientation Forest occurred. A Personal Greeter went out on an assignment to pick up an Inkytootian, who was the first of his kind on Mon-Marg. He was planning to tour the planet and decide if he wanted Inkytootia to take part in The Space Program."

"What happened to them?" Roger asked.

"Well...the Personal Greeter and the Inkytootian never made it out of the forest. Their vector was found just yards away from the Fire Pits. No one knows exactly what happened, but everyone knew who was responsible—the Gorrs. You see, the Mon-Margian atmosphere had made the Gorrs bloodthirsty."

Her final sentence sent chills up Roger's spine.

"So what happened to the Gorrs?" Krin-Tin whispered.

"The king decided that the Gorrs must leave Mon-Marg immediately," Mrs. S. continued. "He ordered Bowgee Berg and Sheriff Jijijian to round all of them up and send them straight back to Gorrinth."

"Did they catch them?" asked Roger.

Mrs. S. shuffled in her seat and looked at Mr. S. uncomfortably. His sad eyes had a strange, faraway look.

"Well, not before the Gorrs claimed one final victim," Mr. Schleffinschlubb intervened slowly. "They killed Sheriff Jijijian before he could apprehend them."

"What happened?" Roger asked slowly.

"Oh, it was horrible!" Mrs. S. cried out fervently. "They tied the poor soul up and dragged him to the Spitting Cactus Trees near the outskirts of town. They set off about 20 cactus trees and left him for dead. I don't even want to think of it!" She sniffed and grabbed a tissue with one of her arms, dabbing the corners of her sparkling green eyes, where orange teardrops formed in the corners.

"So did they ever capture the Gorrs?" asked Krin-Tin.

"Oh yes, well..." Mrs. S. went on, her voice quivering. "Slee Squarevicky from Planet Urg agreed to become the new sheriff."

"I just met Sheriff Squarevicky today!" Roger said.

"What a dear soul. A real lifesaver!" Mrs. S. continued. "Anyway, what Sheriff Squarevicky uncovered shocked the entire town! He found out that Bowgee Berg had been working with the Gorrs all along and was plotting to kill the king and take over the planet!"

"I thought that only good creatures were allowed in The Space Program," Krin-Tin remarked. "If the Gorrs were such troublemakers, then why were they welcome here in the first place?"

"Well, you see, Krin-Tin, at that time the king's assistant was in charge of selecting members for the program. The theory goes that Berg knew the Gorrs were evil and would be perfect partners in crime. That is why he brought them to Mon-Marg. But after he was arrested, everything changed. The Space Committee was formed, splitting the power up and holding a lottery to determine who should become a member of The Space Program."

"Who exactly was the king's assistant?" asked Krin-Tin.

"Back then the king's assistant was the town's only link to the king. He was a resident of Mon-Marg who used several different disguises to protect his identity. This way he could go back and forth freely from the volcano, choosing new members for the program and relaying any information the king wished to impart to the citizens. He also had the only key to the underwater volcano gates. He was allowed to travel freely around the universe and scout out new planets, and was the king's oldest and most trustworthy friend. Now he sits in the town jail alone, exactly where he deserves to be!" Mrs. S.

shouted resentfully, forgetting herself momentarily.

"What a rotten hooligan! A malefactor responsible for wicked deviltry!" Mr. S. chimed in furiously.

"Did he ever show his face?" asked Roger.

"Not really. Since he had full access to the king's volcano, as well as all the coordinates and secrets of space travel, not many were allowed to know who he was. It would be a terrible tragedy if any of the information got around. His identity must always remain a secret. He knows too much. Plus, before he was arrested, the scoundrel hid the key to the underwater volcano gates somewhere in town. To this day, nobody knows where." She shook her head sadly.

"So what happened to the Gorrs?" Krin-Tin asked impatiently.

"Sheriff Squarevicky finally caught up with them and shipped them back to Gorrinth. And that's the end of that story." Mrs. S. finished abruptly and stood up, turning her back to them. Roger thought he noticed her shoulders slump just slightly. But when she turned around, she had regained her composure. The rosy flush returned to her cheeks, and she stood up straight, grabbing dishes from the table with all of her arms and tossing them into the sink.

"Don't worry yourselves, boys. That is all ancient Mon-Margian history. The planet is a very safe place now. We aren't going to let a few rotten Goola eggs spoil the whole carton, are we?" she chuckled.

The two of them nodded in agreement. But Roger couldn't help hearing a crackle of uncertainty in her voice, and he wondered if she was telling them everything she knew about those rotten Goola eggs.

□ □ □ □ □ □ □ □ □ □ □

That night Roger had a difficult time falling asleep. After much tossing and turning, he just lay there in the darkness, gazing out window at the peaceful night and trying to ignore the loud hick-honking that floated down from the upper bunk.

The sound of stirring leaves outside caused Roger to rise just in time to see a black shadow pass fluidly by his window, followed by mumbled whispers. A wave of fear pulsed through him. Why was someone out there this late at night?

Slowly pulling back the covers, Roger got up and tiptoed over to the window. He leaned out cautiously, looking toward the dark footpath—surrounded by bristling bushes and hedges. Roger scanned the area, looking for a sign of life…and then he found one. Nestled in the bushes across the path from his window, two shining eyes stared directly at him, glaring ominously in the reflected moonlight. It took him a while to be absolutely sure that what he was looking at were actually eyes—but when they blinked, all doubt quickly subsided.

What disturbed Roger most was the way the eyes seemed to be fixed on him, unwavering in their direction. He stood there by the window, peering back, too frightened to move. The eyes held Roger's gaze, dully blinking for a few more minutes. Then with a rustling sound, they disappeared, blending into the shadows. Roger promptly slammed the window, yanked the curtains over it, and dove back under the covers.

Although the curtains were drawn and Krin-Tin's hick-honking had eased, he couldn't sleep at all that night. He wondered what was lurking out there—and what exactly it had been looking for. Deep inside, Roger knew the answer. And no matter how hard he tried to shake the feeling—it just wouldn't leave.

It had been looking for him.

Chapter Ten

THE GOLDEN GINGERBREAD COOKIE AND THE GREEN-HAIRED GIRL

The orange morning sun shone across the glittering landscape as Roger and Krin-Tin walked down the mountain path on their first day of school. They encountered many other children, hopping, floating, crawling, springing, rolling, and walking along. Roger took a deep breath of the crisp air, which felt pure and clean in his lungs, and he smelled the faint, sweet fragrance of flowers. They arrived at a four-way crossroad where they nearly collided with two children approaching from the other direction. Neither pair had seen the other coming because of a large, mossy tree overhanging the path.

"Whoa!" cried Roger, tripping over Krin-Tin to avoid bumping into them.

"Heeeeeey!" cried the other boy, who resembled a stocky gingerbread cookie made from breathtaking gold. The boy had two golden antennae on his head that swung back and forth with his every movement. His large nose and black eyes were set close together on his round face.

"You gotta watch the coat, bud. Don't you know that this is gen-u-ine Flintosaurus fur?" The gingerbread cookie smoothed his long, furry white coat.

"Sorry," said Roger, taking note of the boy's haughtiness. "We didn't see you guys coming."

Roger glanced over at the gingerbread cookie's companion. Staring back at him was an almost human-looking girl with smooth pink skin and big green, almond-shaped eyes framed by long lashes and delicate brows. She had an angular face and a small, pointed nose. Her curly green hair matched her eyes and was swept off her face by a shimmering barrette. She wore a shiny silver dress and boots to match.

"That's quite all-righty, bud," said the golden boy. "Why don't you guys walk with us to school? This is this your first year here, right?"

Roger and Krin-Tin nodded.

"My name is Zinkie Melou, and this is Glacindia Garlian," the cookie announced as he swaggered along. "She's from Gree-X."

"Is this your first year here also?" Roger asked.

Zinkie scrunched his golden face in disgust. "Tsk," he scoffed. "No way. I was born here. I'm full-blooded Mon-Margian," he said with pride. "It's just my first year at this school. Glacindia came here at the beginning of summer."

"Well, I'm Roger Webb, and this is my roommate, Krin-Tin Nik..."

"My father is a Space Director, and he's on the Space Committee," Zinkie interrupted rudely. Glacindia rolled her eyes.

Zinkie ignored her and kept talking. "My mother is a professor at Zirgon High. We live on the Top Tier. I've been here forever. I'm a full-blooded Mon-Margian," he said, just in case anyone had missed it the first time.

Roger felt a nudge from behind. He looked back and saw Krin-Tin shake his head and make a mocking face at Zinkie. Glacindia strolled quietly ahead, clutching her books with slender fingers as her green curls bounced and her sparkly barrette gleamed in the sun.

"So...yeah," Zinkie rambled on. "If any of you need to know anything about the planet or the town or The Space Program, you can just come to me. Everyone else does," he said with mock boredom, rolling his eyes. He turned around, facing Roger and Krin-Tin as he walked backwards. Roger observed that Zinkie's legs were too short for his stout body, and his webbed feet were far too big for his legs.

"Let me guess…you're from Earth." Zinkie pointed at Roger. "And you're from A-Zarg." He pointed at Krin-Tin. "Right?" he asked.

"How did you know?" asked Krin-Tin, seemingly impressed.

"I told you, pal. I've been here forever…and I've seen everything," he said with an arrogant smirk, adding, "Ick Juf Bludjick Forlfen."

"What's that supposed to mean?" Krin-Tin asked, frowning.

"It's Mon-Margian for 'Been there…done that.' If ya stick around long enough, you'll learn how to break the Language Decoder barrier and speak Mon-Margian, too."

"So, what's a Flintosaurus?" asked Roger, staring with disdain at the long fur coat Zinkie wore.

"It's only like the most rare and elegant Mon-Margian animal there is. Do you even know how much this cost me?" Zinkie asked, pointing to his glorious attire. Roger personally thought it looked disgusting, as if Zinkie was wearing an oversized white rat.

"Don't you mean how much it cost your father, Zinkie?" Glacindia spoke up. Her voice was low and calm, and Roger noticed a sly grin cross her face as she winked at him. Zinkie became flustered and mumbled something about girls-not-knowing-what-they-were-talking-about. Then he finally shut his big, golden mouth.

They reached the edge of the schoolyard, said good-bye and went their separate ways. Roger felt a wave of joy as he realized he'd already made three friends on Mon-Marg. That was three more than he ever had on Earth, even if one of them was a stuck-up, fur-wearing braggart. But even though Zinkie was a show-off and a know-it-all, Roger sensed a nice side that he had buried somewhere under all that Flintosaurus fur.

□ □ □ □ □ □ □ □ □ □ □

Roger had a frustrating morning trying to find his way around. He was late for three classes, burst in on a teacher's meeting by mistake, and at one point found himself in the girls' washroom, where a shrieking girl from the planet Redexa angrily chased him out. She had shock-red hair and four mouths, each screaming different things. Needless to say, Roger's ears were ringing all morning. He was understandably relieved when it was finally time for lunch.

Upon entering the cafeteria, Roger grabbed a tray and some silverware and took a place at the end of the line. He tried to catch sight of Krin-Tin but couldn't see much because the boy in the next line was about seven feet tall with bristles all over his body that blocked his view.

"C'MON!!!! MOVE IT ALONG DOWN THERE!!!!" A loud shriek from the front of the line interrupted Roger's thoughts, further shattering his eardrums. It was the lunch lady, Mrs. Xander-Wixx. She came from the planet Jazzarex and resembled a giant bird, complete with winglike arms, brightly colored feathers, and a sharp beak. She squinted at Roger with tiny red eyes, and tapped her long talons defensively.

"Well, I haven't got all day! Let's go! What'll it be?" she squawked.

Roger looked over his choices. The sign above the counter read:

LUNCH MENU
HOOBERMELON
DANCING TOAD LIVER
ZIPPY FISH STEW
MON-MARGIAN TURTLE CUTLETS
SUZUKI EGGS

Roger gulped miserably as he looked over his options. The suzuzi eggs had a grayish hue and moldy blue spots. The zippy fish stew looked like chunks of garbage floating in bubbling slime and smelled like rotten cabbage, and the Mon-Margian turtle cutlets reminded him of slabs of concrete. He couldn't even look at the dancing toad liver for fear of losing his breakfast. None of the food looked remotely appetizing to Roger, but Mrs. Xander-Wixx was getting impatient.

"WELL? WHAT IS IT? I'VE GOT A WHOLE LINE OF HUNGRY MOUTHS BEHIND YOU. HURRY IT UP, CURLY-JOE!" she screeched, her beak snapping.

"Ummm...I'll just have a slice of Hoobermelon and some Suzuzi eggs please," said Roger hesitantly, wondering if there was anything on the entire planet of Mon-Marg that he might like to eat.

The bird lady scowled at Roger, dipped her serving spoon into the pile of revolting eggs, and slopped some on his plate. She grabbed a slice of Hoobermelon and threw it on top of the eggs. After pecking the prices into the scanner, she motioned at Roger to slide his ID/money card through. Earlier that morning, Mr. Schleffinschlubb had handed Roger and Krin-Tin each a small card and explained, "This card represents your monetary status reflected by the amount that we, as benefactors of your welfare, see fit to distribute. When the time comes that you discover the card is void of worth, we shall augment it to suit your fiscal needs." Mrs. Schleffinschlubb then translated his words by saying, "Use these money cards for your school lunches or any other small things you might need. When you run out of money, we'll deposit more."

Roger barely got done sliding the card when he heard Mrs. Xander-Wixx's piercing screech: "NNNNNEEEEEXXTTTTT!" He stepped into the dining area and looked for a familiar face. Back on

Earth, lunch had always been his least favorite part of the day. Every day he ended up alone at a large table, while all the other kids gathered in groups to laugh and tell stories. Roger began to feel the familiar sting of rejection when suddenly he spotted Krin-Tin's gangly green arm waving at him from across the crowded room. Then he saw Zinkie and Glacindia at the same table turn and wave at him too. Roger bit his lip to keep from smiling, and hurried over to the table to sit down.

"Hey, guys."

"What'cha got there, bud?" asked Zinkie.

"Suzuzi eggs and Hoobermelon." Roger stuck out his tongue. "That lunch lady was mean!"

"The Xander-Witch!" Zinkie scoffed. "That stuff looks disgusting."

"I was warned never to touch that stuff!" said Glacindia, reaching into her lunch box, which had the cast of the show *Journey to Vexicon Galaxy* on it, and pulling out a neatly wrapped sandwich. Something blue and gooey held the bread together.

"Well, I'm not sure the Schleffinschlubbs would make us anything much better," laughed Krin-Tin as he pushed some yellow slop around his plate.

"I know what you mean," said Roger as he took a bite of Hoobermelon and winced at its sour flavor. The sticky juice ran down his arm and immediately hardened into a waxy brown gel. "Gross," he said, chipping away the congealed juice.

"Oh, no! Quick! Duck!" Glacindia said.

"What?" Roger asked. Before he could turn around, he felt the table begin to shake. It started as a distant tremor, and then became progressively louder and more forceful until everything on the table was rattling and shaking. Soon the BOOM...BOOM...BOOM was directly behind them.

"Tuber Bleck," said Zinkie disgustedly.

Tuber Bleck was a blobby purple boy from the Planet Morvidox. His round, fleshy head sat right on top of his mountainous body, smothering any evidence of a neck. Three small white horns stuck out from the very center of his head, two bulging eyes protruding from his face like marbles, and his fleshy lips resembled a fish. Roger watched as Tuber lumbered over to their lunch table, swaying and jiggling with every movement. He slapped his enormous tray of food down across from Roger and squeezed himself into the bench.

"Hey, y'all," he grunted.

"Hey Tuber, this is Krin-Tin and Roger," Zinkie said, nodding his head towards the two of them. "And you already know Glacindia."

Tuber nodded at Krin-Tin and Roger. "And how are you, Miss Garlian?" Tuber smiled bashfully, revealing a row of rotting teeth as he struggled to turn towards Glacindia.

"Ugh," said Glacindia snobbishly.

Roger was filled with revulsion as Tuber opened a cardboard box and hundreds of tiny, spider-like insects spilled out. They were black and furry, and each one had about 18 legs. As they scurried in different directions, Tuber agilely scooped them up in his pudgy hand and shoved them greedily into his mouth. Roger began to feel sick listening to the crunching noise Tuber made as he chewed, licking his fat lips after each successful capture.

"W–w–what are those!?" stammered Krin-Tin, his green skin fading to a sickly lime color.

"These are Crawling Wendels. They're delicious...wanna try some?" Tuber held out a heaping handful of bugs, some scrambling down his arm and onto the table.

"No thanks!" they all said in unison.

"Suit yourself," Tuber shrugged, reaching for another scampering handful.

Roger looked down at his Suzuzi eggs and heard his stomach growl loudly from hunger pains. Surprised, Tuber looked up at Roger from his box of bugs and grunted: "Do you have a monster in your stomach also?"

Chapter Eleven

IN THE BRIARS

Months had passed since Roger's landing in Orientation Forest. He was adapting well to living on another planet—the odd creatures, the magical scenery, and even the unappetizing food. Krin-Tin, Zinkie, and Glacindia had become his closest friends, and Roger found that living with the Schleffinschlubbs was very comforting. Roger was still uneasy about the mysterious eyes that had been watching him and the ominous feeling he'd had in the forest on his first night. For the most part, though, he pushed those thoughts from his mind and focused on enjoying The Space Program.

Dear Mom,

I'm writing to tell you that I got your letter. I love it here at Newton's Academy of Scientific Children. Nahi-Nahi is a beautiful place, and I'm learning a lot about the Loggerhead Sea Turtles and the cycles of the moon. I'm not as afraid of turtles as I once was, and I realize now that even though they are ugly and scary-looking, they should be treated with kindness. Besides the turtles, I'm doing well in all of my classes and have made three new friends who I think you'd like. I miss you very much, and I hope that you are doing okay back home.

Love,
Roger

P.S. The food here isn't very good. I miss your lunches.

P.P.S. I'm sorry about Mr. Chuckles and the poker game. Do wine stains come out of carpets?

Roger had five minutes between classes and wanted to get to the mailbox across the street before missing the weekly 3:00 deadline. Slipping out the front door of the school, he ran across the playground, crossed the empty street to the mailbox, and dropped the letter inside. He was surprised when he heard a faint mumbling coming from the cluster of briars next to the mailbox.

The briars were tall and dense, and they had knotted branches with thick, sharp thorns. Roger couldn't imagine how anyone or anything could be among them by choice, so he stopped and listened. The mumbling had ceased, and there was silence. He shrugged and turned away when he sensed movement in the briars, then a pained and desperate voice called out, "Pleeeeaaassse...Help..."

Someone was trapped in the briars! Roger stared in disbelief. He moved closer to the spot where the voice had originated and listened. Again, silence.

"Hello?" said Roger. "Who's there?"

More silence. Roger thought that whoever was stuck in there must be in a lot of pain, judging from the sharp thorns, and he wasn't sure what he should do. When he noticed more movement deep within the tangled foliage, he bent down and peered through the branches, but they were too dense.

"Do you want me to get help?" he yelled out.

"No...don't leeeavve mee heeere..." the voice whispered fearfully. "You...you mustn't leave me here!"

"Well, how can I help you?" Roger called out.

Then to Roger's horror, the same sickly voice whispered menacingly, "I've been waiting for you...Roger Webb." And before Roger could react, a wrinkled and bony hand shot out from the briars. Spotted with tufts of thick white fur, its grisly fingers had

long yellow claws. It lunged and grabbed him—the briars shaking violently as the creature struggled to break free.

A scream stuck deep in his throat as Roger broke away and began sprinting towards school. He ran as fast as he could across the street, across the playground, and through the main doors of the school. Once inside, he nervously peered out. There was nothing behind him—all was quiet and empty. Shaken, he hurried off to his Suns and Moons class.

Sliding into his chair at the back of the room, Roger was still out of breath and dizzy from running so fast. The Suns and Moons teacher, Mr. Boolaboo, was busy drawing a chart of lunar eclipses on the presentation board and hadn't noticed Roger sneak in.

Still trembling, he took a few deep breaths to calm down and think about what had happened. Something had been following him—he was absolutely sure of it now. First he'd had the strange feeling that first night in Orientation Forest with Gwan. Then he had seen something staring at him from outside his bedroom. This time, its gnarled hand had actually grabbed him! It said it had been waiting for him, and it had known Roger's name!

But who could be after me? What would anyone want from me? Scenarios flashed through his mind. Had he done anything since he had arrived on Mon-Marg that would make someone want to harm him? Did he, as an Earthling, own something that another alien might value? Nothing made sense.

His brow furrowed, Roger sat deep in concentration. Then, like a lightning bolt, the answer came to him. Keeping one eye on Mr. Boolaboo, Roger reached down to his backpack and slowly unzipped the secret side pocket. There it was, just as he had left it—the blue box that he found in the forest on Earth.

Chapter Twelve

ADVENTURES ON A RAINY DAY

Plip...plip...plip...Roger awoke one Saturday morning to the familiar sound of raindrops hitting the awning outside his bedroom window. He hastily threw off the covers and jumped out of bed. "Krin-Tin. Wake up!"

Roger tugged at the sheets on the upper bunk where his roommate hick-honked noisily in a deep sleep. Krin-Tin sat up grumpily.

"What? Why are you up so early? It's the weekend!"

"It's raining out! Don't you hear it? Just like on Earth! C'mon, let's go outside," Roger yelled excitedly. He had been away from Earth for months now and was feeling very sentimental towards anything that reminded him of home. He grabbed his boots and bounded down the stairs two at a time.

"And what are you doing up so early?" Mrs. S. calmly asked Roger, simultaneously flipping through the pages of the *Explorer*, sipping her morning drink of sap, and readjusting the pink rubber band that held her braid together.

"I'm going outside! Don't you hear the rain?" Roger asked, rummaging through the closet for his raincoat.

"Most certainly. We are experiencing tempestuous showers today," said Mr. S. absentmindedly, deeply engrossed in his paper. "It's a shame you boys will have to remain inside the dwelling..." Trailing off, he turned to Mrs. S. "Did you perceive the price of Hoobermelons is rising?"

Roger found his raincoat and headed towards the door. He

gripped the handle and started to turn it when suddenly four of Mrs. Schleffinschlubbs' arms were wrapped around him, pulling him back.

"Wait!" she screamed. Roger teetered and almost lost his balance. "Where is your umbrella?"

"Aww, I don't need an umbrella, Mrs. S. I have this raincoat, see?" said Roger, pulling away from her grasp and moving towards the door. He gripped the handle again and pulled the door open. This time Mrs. Schleffinschlubb knocked him right off his feet.

Roger sat on the ground, dazed and looking out the open door. He couldn't believe what he was seeing! Falling from the dark green sky were millions of tiny rocks! They sprinkled down from swirling gray storm clouds for miles, clicking and clattering, bouncing and scattering everywhere!

"Now do you see why you need an umbrella?" said Mrs. S., pointing to the steel umbrella in the corner of the front hallway. Roger slowly got up, watching the rocks pittering and pattering as they hit the ground. Disappointed, he shut the door just as Krin-Tin came clomping down the stairs.

"What's all the noise about?" he asked, rubbing his sleepy eyes.

"Roger has witnessed his first meteor shower, Krin-Tin," said Mrs. S. with a smile. "Do you have meteor showers on A-Zarg?"

"Of course!" said Krin-Tin.

Roger scowled and sat on the couch gloomily. Now what was there to do? There was bad weather, and no one would be outside. He didn't want to spend his whole weekend inside the house doing nothing. Suddenly the Videophone rang, and Roger jumped to answer it. It was Zinkie. He and Glacindia were hanging out at his house, and he wanted to know, since it was raining, if Roger and Krin-Tin wanted to come over and watch TV and, oh...also...see all his new toys.

Roger was thrilled for an opportunity to get out of the house. After much debating, Krin-Tin reluctantly agreed to go, even though he was allergic to meteor showers and would miss his favorite TV show, *The Milky Way Group*.

□ □ □ □ □ □ □ □ □ □ □

Grasping their steel umbrellas, Roger and Krin-Tin walked up the mountain. The rocks seemed to be coming down with less force than before, and the swirling storm clouds were breaking up a bit.

Roger and Krin-Tin had never been to the Top Tier. When they reached it, they were surprised to see a silver gate guarded by a creature with a long scaly body, and huge black eyes that shifted continuously back and forth as if he were watching for something. He was obviously from Planet Urg, just like Sheriff Squarevicky, but Roger and Krin-Tin soon found that he lacked the friendly disposition of the sheriff. When the Urggian saw them approaching, he stuck out his lizard tongue.

"Can I help you boysss?"

"Yes. We're here to visit Zinkie Melou," Krin-Tin spoke up.

The creature slid out of his stone chair and slowly moved over to the intercom system, keeping his untrusting eyes on the two of them. Roger noticed that even as the Urggian leaned over to speak into the intercom, they could not escape his ominous gaze, and he began to feel very ill at ease.

"Who can I sssay isss here?"

"Roger and Krin-Tin," they said in unison. The guard pressed a few buttons with spoon-like hands and waited until someone answered.

"Yesss, Mr. Melou. I have a Roger and a Krin-Tin here to sssee you...Yesss...Uh-huh...Very well then," he hissed.

The guard pushed another button, and the gate inched open slowly. Roger and Krin-Tin moved quickly through, glad to get away from the spooky guard.

"That guard was scary," Krin-Tin said out of the corner of his mouth.

They finally reached Zinkie's house, which was beautiful indeed. It was chiseled straight from the mountain and rose up three stories. The polished surface of the rock shone like blue ice. Roger reached up and rang the doorbell, setting off a series of low, echoing chimes.

Zinkie showed up a minute later wearing brand new Tarsek Wane shoes. Tarsek Wane was the most successful fashion designer on Mon-Marg. Only important and wealthy Mon-Margians could afford his line of clothing, and he was even said to have designed the king's wardrobe.

"Welcome, welcome," said Zinkie. "Come in."

The two of them snapped their steel umbrellas shut and followed Zinkie into the enormous house.

They walked through a spacious kitchen into the game room, where Glacindia was stretched out on a couch. She was flipping through the pages of a teen magazine called *Stars in the Stars* that had a picture of her favorite actor, Marcius Mellvain, on the cover. The ending credits of *The Milky Way Group* were playing on a towering TV wall.

"Well, it's about time!" she said crossly, as the boys entered the room. She scowled at Roger and Krin-Tin, straightening the barrette in her curly green hair.

"Well, there was a meteor shower, and then we got stopped by that creepy guard," explained Roger. "He's Urggian, just like Sheriff

Squarevicky, right?"

"Very observant, my friend," said Zinkie sarcastically. Roger suddenly wished that he could find some of the other Earthlings on Mon-Marg. He saw some once in awhile, but most of them were older. He wanted to be able to talk to someone his own age about The Space Program and life on Mon-Marg.

"So why is he so weird and cranky? The sheriff is a lot nicer than he is!" said Krin-Tin, brushing bits of rock from his recently shined boots.

"Beats me," said Zinkie. "Probably because he's stuck being a guard on top of this mountain. He really doesn't like to leave his post too often; it's way too risky for him."

"What do you mean, too risky?" asked Roger.

"Well, all Urggians are allergic to their own reflection. If they catch even the slightest glimpse of themselves, they freeze up and die. That's why they make such good guards and policemen and stuff. They have to be very aware of their surroundings."

"That explains why the guard didn't take his eyes off us," said Krin-Tin.

"Yeah, that was weird," Roger said, feeling very lucky to be just a regular Earthling, with no major limitations. It was still strange to discover the many differences among Mon-Margian species.

"I'm allergic to a lot of things," Krin-Tin chimed in. "Feathers, bugs, some kinds of water…"

"Anyway, not to worry," interrupted Zinkie. "You guys are here now."

He started to walk and forcefully hit his foot against a stone table. "Ouuuuch!" he yelped dramatically, hopping up and down on one stocky gold leg and clutching his brand new Tarsek Wane'd foot in his webbed hands. Roger saw immediately what he was doing and refused to comment on the shoes.

"Are you okay?" Roger said blandly, crossing his arms.

"Yeah...I think so," Zinkie panted, scrunching his nose and rubbing his foot, making sure to display the side with the label on it.

Glacindia was fed up with his show. "He wants you guys to notice that he got new Tarsek Wane shoes," she said, arching one eyebrow and grinning wickedly.

Zinkie immediately straightened up, miraculously recovered from his debilitating foot injury.

"Shut up, Glacindia! I do not. I mean really, what's the big deal anyway? I have, like, at least three other pairs anyway," he snapped, turning a copper color as he blushed.

Glacindia stared back at him, unconvinced.

"So," said Zinkie, ready to change the subject, "do you guys want to go see my room?"

"Oh, goodie!" yelled Glacindia as she jumped up from the couch. "It's about time!"

□ □ □ □ □ □ □ □ □ □ □

After a few hours of rummaging through Zinkie's plethora of toys and games, Glacindia pouted. "I'm bored."

"What else is new?" Zinkie answered distractedly, as he battered away on Krin-Tin during their Virtual Boxing match.

"Oww!" screamed Krin-Tin, catching a hard left jab to his virtual chin.

Roger sat next to the screen, trying to figure out a patternless puzzle from the planet Redexa.

"Should we show them your dad's office?" Glacindia smiled slyly, putting down Zinkie's Hubbert the Spaceman doll, whose fur she had just shorn with a pair of electric scissors.

"Yowch!" Krin-Tin cried as he virtually hit the floor with a crunch. Zinkie stood over him, victorious. He thought for a minute, and then said with a hint of mischief in his voice, "Can you guys keep a secret?"

Chapter Thirteen

THE OFFICE OF DR. MELOU

Zinkie slowly pushed open a heavy stone door, peered around it, and flipped on the light switch. The others followed close behind. The sizable room was filled from ceiling to floor with shelves of books and papers, plaques and medals.

On the desk was a framed photograph of Dr. Melou standing next to King Gloob—a floating, transparent blue blob. The picture had been taken at Dr. Melou's Space Director initiation party. In another photo, all of the Space Directors had gathered for a group shot. Roger smiled when he spotted Dr. Von Tibbetson in the back row. His glasses were crooked, his toothless smile was broad, and he was looking away from the camera.

Roger continued looking at Dr. Melou's awards and pictures as Zinkie and Glacindia rummaged through a huge closet. Krin-Tin sat, looking fragile in an oversized chair lined with pink spotted Flintosaurus fur.

"I really hope that no one's home, Zinkie. I'm sure your dad would kill us if he caught us in here," said Krin-Tin from across the room, shaking his head anxiously.

"Fraidy cat!" Glacindia taunted.

"Awww, don't worry about it, bud," Zinkie said, digging through boxes. "My father is on a very important mission. He won't be home for days. And my mother's out shopping—she won't be home for weeks."

Roger wandered over to the big desk and sat in the swivel chair, turning around a few times. Between spins he noticed a blue folder

sticking out from underneath the desk and bent over to pick it up.
On the front of the folder were the words:

OFFICIAL SPACE DIRECTOR BUSINESS AND NEWS CLIPS

Roger stared down at the folder. He knew that he really should-
n't be nosing around in official Space Director's business, but his
curiosity got the best of him. Slowly he opened it up and looked down
at the first page. It was a newspaper clipping from *The Explorer*
dated six years ago.

SPITTING CACTUS SET OFF. GORRS SUSPECTED

The next page was another clipping:

ROGUE GORRS TOY WITH TRAFFIC LIGHTS—
TWO VECTORS IN COLLISION—MINOR INJURIES

Under that, Roger found an official memo dated a month later,
which had CONFIDENTIAL stamped on the top. He knew he
shouldn't be reading it, but by then he was well past the point
of reason.

ATTENTION ALL SPACE DIRECTORS AND PERSONAL GREETERS

Re: Missing Personal Greeter and Assignment

All Space Directors must be on alert for suspicious activity in and around
the town of Zirgon, including Handucian Fields and Orientation Forest. On the third
moon of the sixth cycle, Personal Greeter Buzzo Yindow set out to greet his assignment, "New Creature Inkytootian." Neither emerged from Orientation Forest as
scheduled. Vehicle was later recovered near the Fire Pits. Neither Yindow nor
Inkytootian have been seen since. Both are presumed dead. Gorrs suspected.

—Bowgee Berg, Assistant to the King

Roger turned to the next announcement—another clipping from *The Explorer*. The headline read:

SHERIFF JIJIJIAN KILLED. HUNT FOR GORRS TO BEGIN.

Finally the last item in the folder was another confidential memo.

ATTENTION ALL SPACE DIRECTORS AND PERSONAL GREETERS—
ALL POINTS BULLETIN

Re: King's Assistant

As you all are aware, King Gloob's assistant, Bowgee Berg, was arrested and found guilty of conspiring with the Gorrs. Please be aware that only four of the Gorrs have been captured and sent back to Gorrinth. Be on the lookout for the fifth Gorr. He is extremely dangerous and may be in possession of the key to the underwater volcano gate. Please be discreet with this knowledge. Do not alarm the public.

—Sheriff Slee Squarevicky

Roger dropped the folder, which landed smack on the floor.

"What was that?" asked Krin-Tin, rising from his chair and walking towards Roger. "What's the matter?"

"It's the Gorr," Roger whispered. "He's still here!"

"What are you talking about?" asked Glacindia, collecting the folder from the floor and flipping through it.

"Everything's right there!" said Roger. "I knew I was being followed ever since I got here...and look!" he said, pointing to the last article. "It says right there that the fifth Gorr was never found!" Zinkie sauntered over to the group and boorishly grabbed the article from Glacindia's hand.

"Lemme see that!" He scanned the article. "So what? What's this got to do with you?"

"Zinkie!" Roger yelled. "I told you that weird things have been happening to me ever since I arrived here! I know I've been followed, and now I've found out that the fifth Gorr was never found!"

"But even if he was still alive, what would he want with you?" asked Glacindia, standing with her arms crossed, her thin eyebrows raised. "You don't know where the missing key is...or do you?" All three of them studied Roger.

"Of course I don't!" Roger screamed. "How would I know where the...?" And then he stopped. The room started to spin, and he felt like he might faint.

"What's wrong, Roger? You look sick!" Krin-Tin said.

Roger slowly reached into his backpack and produced the blue box. He held it out with a shaking hand.

"Maybe I do know where the key is," he gulped. It suddenly made sense to him. The key was in the blue box, and the fifth Gorr knew it!

"I remember there were big hunts for the key after that happened. The whole town came out to search every day until it got dark. They told us the king's assistant probably hid it somewhere in town before he was arrested. Nobody ever found it, though," Zinkie said, seizing the box from Roger and shaking it.

"But what if, before he was arrested, he planted the key some-where for the Gorr to find? That's it! He hid it in a Transport Bubble! It must have fallen out accidentally in the forest near my house. The Gorr figured out that I have it, and now he's stalking me!" Roger gasped.

"Well, I personally think you're crazy. Everyone knows the king's assistant either destroyed the key, or it went into the Fire Pits—just where I'm sure this fifth Gorr ended up," Zinkie said. "Mon-Marg is a safe place. You're just imagining things."

Roger's mind was racing. He was convinced he'd figured everything out. It all made sense—the feelings of being followed, the eyes outside his window, the creature in the briars. It had to be the Gorr!

"Well, let's forget all this nonsense and go have some fun!" said Glacindia, her mischievous green eyes gleaming as she held something behind her back.

"You found it?" Zinkie asked excitedly.

"Yep!" yelled Glacindia, as she pulled out a strange-looking object from behind her back. It was a mask with a small mouthpiece, and goggles and tubes attached to it.

"What is that thing?" asked Krin-Tin, a disapproving look crossing his face.

"It's my father's very own Mon-Margian Liquid Lung," said Zinkie proudly.

"What are we going to do with it?" asked Roger, still reeling from his discovery.

"What else, silly?" said Glacindia. "We're going to explore Lake Fuddle Mudd!" She jumped up and down, clapping her delicate hands.

"Oooh, no!!!" Krin-Tin shook his head insistently. "No way...not me! Do you know how much trouble we can get into if we're caught?"

Chapter Fourteen

THE MUDDSHIRE BOGGLINGS

The meteor shower had ended. The dark storm clouds were swirling pink mists again, and the sky regained its mystical green color. Zinkie Melou sat at the edge of Lake Fuddle Mudd, tossing stones into the dark churning water. Plip...plop...the stones skidded and kerplunked as they hit the murky surface and sank.

"I heard there are monsters down there," Zinkie said.

"I heard there's a sand fog. It pulls you down, and you can never get out," Glacindia said.

"I heard the water might be poisoned," Roger said.

"I've got a really bad feeling about this, you guys," Krin-Tin added.

"So who's gonna go first?" Glacindia said, tugging on Roger's blond curls. "B-o-i-n-g!" she added.

"Why don't you go first, Krin-Tin?" said Zinkie.

"Uh-uh," said Krin-Tin. "I told you I'm not going into that lake. None of us know what's down there, and I have no idea how my allergies will react to that water. Plus we could get into a lot of trouble." He kicked a stone and let out a stifled honk.

"Aww, what a baby," said Zinkie, standing up and strutting towards the group. "Fine, gimme that thing!" He took the device from Glacindia. "I'll go. It's no big deal," he added with false bravado.

The others watched as Zinkie affixed the goggles over his eyes, put the tube up to his mouth, and attached the cord into his utility belt. Roger couldn't help giggling at the sight of Zinkie, the golden swamp monster.

"O-b-kay-b, h-bere, I-ba g-bo!" He jumped into the bubbling lake with a giant splash. The last thing Roger saw was Zinkie's waving antennae just before they disappeared into the water. Roger and Glacindia ran over to the edge and stared into the murky abyss. Their reflections were odd and distorted from the rippling current.

Roger turned to look at Krin-Tin, who was pouting on a large rock behind them. He had his green conehead in his hands, and he was kicking his oversized boots against the rock.

"I'm really worried about the Gorr," Roger quietly confessed to Glacindia. "I know you guys don't believe me, but I'm sure he's been following me."

"But Roger, that business with the Gorrs happened years ago. If the fifth Gorr were still here, don't you think someone would have seen him by now?" Glacindia asked. "He must have died in the Fire Pits and taken the key with him." She skipped another stone across the lake.

"But what if he didn't? What if he's still alive and looking for the key? What if the king's assistant told him which Transport Bubble he hid it in, and he figured out that I have it?"

"But no one is allowed to speak to the king's assistant, Roger. He's in jail. If the Gorr knew where the key was, he would have found it years ago," Glacindia answered.

"Well, either way, I need to find out what's in that blue box."

After some time had passed, Zinkie's big gold head resurfaced, and he dragged himself out of the lake. Pulling off the device, he plopped down, exhausted and soaking wet.

"Well?" cried Glacindia, "What was it like?"

"It was okay," said Zinkie, catching his breath. "It was kind of hard to see through the sand fog. There were a bunch of sand dunes and shells down there. It was boring, actually. Who's going next?" He stared at them demandingly.

Roger and Glacindia looked at each other and shrugged. "You go," they said in unison, pointing at each other.

"Okay, fine. I'll go," Roger said reluctantly. He took the Liquid Lung from Zinkie and stood by the edge, contemplating the forbidden water. Suddenly he felt very nervous. Roger had a strong feeling that there might be much more skulking around beneath the surface of the lake than Zinkie had seen.

Counting to three, Roger plunged in. The cold water engulfed him as he rapidly sank to the bottom. His feet hit the sandy floor with a thud, and he was surprised that he could breathe effortlessly. It was very peaceful below the surface—tiny bubbles were everywhere, and there was a thick layer of sand floating around, making it extremely difficult to see.

Looking around, Roger realized that what Zinkie had said was true. There were lots of shells, and large sloping sand dunes dominated the underwater seascape. He swam right up next to the smooth hills, pausing to reach down and grab some rainbow-colored shells, that were slightly buried in the sandy floor.

Without warning, something seized Roger from behind. His underwater scream sounded like a gurgle. Roger turned to face a slithering creature with the face of a rat—beady red eyes, a sharp nose, long yellow teeth—and the twisting body of a snake, save for a long hairless tail and bony arms. It glided through the water agilely, circling Roger, and studying him intently. Finally the water rat grinned and held out a jagged claw, beckoning him to follow. Roger was afraid, but found himself spellbound. He looked on in morbid curiosity as the creature spoke in a high-pitched, bubbling voice.

"Welcome to the Muddshire Bogg.
We're glad that you are here.
We hope that you can save us from
The danger that is near."

She bowed, flicked her tail, and offered her skeletal arm. Roger stared at her and decided he wasn't about to go anywhere with the dreadful rat. But before he could say no, the creature gripped his arm and escorted him fluidly to the other side of the dunes.

Suddenly white lights appeared, forming a distinct path on the floor of the lake. Looking ahead, Roger saw a sprawling underwater city. Houses made from sand and shells were scattered about randomly. Inhabiting the city were electric rainbow eels, tinkling glassfish, and grinning seahorses. There were sobbing starfish, giant snapping clams, waltzing white lobsters, and spindly jellyfish playing catch with pearls.

It seemed to Roger that everything stopped and stared at him as he entered their realm. Now an entire group of rat-faced snakes swam up and formed a solid ring around him. They chanted in unison:

"Danger, danger from afar.
You must warn the king!
You're followed by the evil star.
Things aren't as they seem!"

Roger stared in amazement. "What do you mean, the evil star?" he sputtered. His voice sounded strange and muffled underwater.

"Warn the king
Before it's late.
There's been a stranger
At the gate!"

"What gate?" Roger asked. Before he got an answer, the Muddshire Boggling whisked him away, stopping abruptly in front of a towering gate that was built into the side of the volcano. Roger gasped at the structure. It was encrusted with diamonds, rubies, emeralds, and twinkling purple amethysts. Running his hands over the smooth surface of the gate and its small keyhole, he suddenly realized that he was looking at the underwater entrance to the king's volcano!

He wondered why the Boggling was showing the gate to him. He looked at the sea rat for an explanation, and she responded with another odd verse.

"Death's in store for the noble sun.
We don't have very long.
The evil star is closing in.
Mon-Marg will soon be gone!"

Again the Boggling silently took Roger by the arm and led him back through the city. As she brought him to the lighted path, a chorus of underwater voices called out to him:

"Good luck…good luck,
There's no more time to waste.
Save our precious Mon-Marg.
Quick! Make haste!"

Roger was then pulled swiftly through the water and deposited back at the scene of his abduction. He had to get back and tell the others what he had seen and heard! His stomach was in knots as he pushed up off the bottom and glided to the surface. Emerging from the lake, Roger saw a pair of boots that were too small to be Krin-Tin's and too old to be Zinkie's. He looked up slowly and faced the owner of the boots—a very angry-looking Sheriff Squarevicky.

Chapter Fifteen

CRIME

Sheriff Squarevicky stood, hands on his hips, staring down at Roger with piercing black eyes. His familiar pleasant expression had morphed into a sneering grimace. Roger sheepishly crawled out of Lake Fuddle Mudd, glancing around for his absent friends. He pulled the Liquid Lung from his head and stood dripping and freezing in front of the irate sheriff, his eyes glued to the ground.

"Well, Mr. Webb?" hissed the sheriff. "I'm sssure my fassse wasss the lassst one you were eggspecting to sssee after resssurfacing from your little ssswim! Wasssn't it?" His voice was hostile.

Roger nodded somberly, unable to look the sheriff in the eye. He knew he was going to get into heaps of trouble—and worse, that he deserved every bit of it. He never should have gone along with Glacindia and Zinkie's plan to explore Lake Fuddle Mudd.

As Roger stood in front of Sheriff Squarevicky, ashamed and frightened, he knew that he couldn't keep what he'd seen a secret. "Sheriff Squarevicky!" he whispered, his voice cracking with fear, "I think I'm in a lot of trouble!"

"You'd better believe you are!" snapped the sheriff. "I'm sssure you know that the crime of being caught in Lake Fuddle Mudd warrantsss a huge punisshment!" He crossed his scaly arms, tapping the fingers of both black-gloved hands as he glared at accusingly at Roger.

"No, sir, you don't understand!" cried Roger. "I'm being followed..." His voice shook and trailed off.

"All right, why don't we talk about it on the way to the ssstation,

Roger," the sheriff said, clutching Roger's arm and dragging him towards his Patrolvector. Pushing Roger into the back seat, he slammed the door behind him. Roger tried to figure out the best way to tell him everything that had happened, step by step, but instead, he just blurted it out all at once.

"I think I'm being followed by the fifth Gorr. When I was on Earth, I found a box in the landing forest, and I think it's the key to the volcano, and the Gorr wants it in order to kill the king and take over the planet somehow, and I don't know what I should do! All I know is that ever since I got to Mon-Marg, something strange has been going on," he said. "On the first night I arrived, someone in Orientation Forest was watching me. Then I saw a pair of eyes outside my bedroom window. Then something was hiding in the briars near the school, and it grabbed me! And today when I went underwater, the Bogglings said the king was in danger, that we're all in danger, and I should warn the king before it's too late. I really don't know who to tell, so I'm telling you! So can you get the message to King Gloob?" Roger was frantic.

"Whooooaaaa...ssslow down, Roger," said the sheriff, pulling the Patrolvector to the side of the road. His calm voice had returned. "What did the Bogglingsss tell you eggsssactly?"

"They told me that someone had been down there and was trying to get into the volcano gate," Roger said excitedly. "They also said that the king was in danger, and that things aren't always what they seem. Something about the death of the noble sun...destroyed by the evil star...and that Mon-Marg would be gone soon if we didn't do something!"

The sheriff sighed. "I think that you should know sssomething about the Muddshire Bogglingsss, Roger," he said sternly. "One reassson that no one is allowed in that lake is that the Bogglingsss don't particularly care for Mon-Margians. They probably told you that ssstory in order to ssscare you off. Yesss?" the sheriff raised his thin eyebrows at Roger.

"Yes," said Roger quietly.

"I'm sssurprissed the Bogglingsss even let you sssee the gate; they are known for fiersssely guarding it. Did any of your little friendsss happen to ssstumble upon the Bogglingsss while they were down there?" asked the sheriff, starting up the Vector again.

"No, sir," said Roger, surprised that the sheriff knew about the other three.

"Yesss," the sheriff nodded. "Your little friendsss ssscattered like Goola Birdsss when they sssaw me coming. Don't worry, I'm going to go to their homesss to have a few wordsss with them alssso. As far as your concernsss about the fifth Gorr, I think you ssshould ssstop worrying about that right now. You are correct. I only caught four of the Gorrsss, but everyone knowsss that the fifth Gorr isss long gone. He couldn't make it here alone, without the othersss."

"But sheriff," Roger interrupted. Digging into his backpack, he pulled out the blue box. "I found this in a landing field on Earth. I think the key to the volcano gate may be in it!"

The sheriff took the box from Roger, then studied and shook it. It made a faint rattling sound. Handing the box back to him, the sheriff said, "Don't be sssilly, Roger. The key isss long gone."

The two rode in silence towards the police station. Roger watched the passing scenery through the window and wished he hadn't followed Zinkie into the lake. He was happy the sheriff had cleared some things up for him, but now he would have to start from the beginning to find out who was following him and why.

His thoughts were interrupted by a loud pounding noise on the side of the vehicle. Looking up, he saw a surprised and frowning Mr. Schleffinschlubb, a bag of groceries in each of his eight arms. The Patrolvector had stopped at a traffic light, and Mr. S. was on his way back from work. Of all the faces to see now, thought Roger, this was the last one he'd hoped for. Only seeing the Gorr himself would have been worse.

Chapter Sixteen

PUNISHMENT

After the Lake Fuddle Mudd incident, Roger, Krin-Tin, Zinkie, and Glacindia were punished for two weeks. Every day after school, they had to sit with other delinquent students in a dingy, run-down room in the basement of the school and write long essays on why they would never go into Lake Fuddle Mudd again, and how extremely sorry they were to disappoint everyone with their lack of judgment and reprehensible behavior.

Sheriff Squarevicky told the Schleffinschlubbs that Roger and Krin-Tin were very lucky that they were not going to be sent back to their home planets after what they did. He reminded them that he would be watching them—if there were any more mischief, they would be expelled from Mon-Marg. Krin-Tin was especially bothered by the punishment. He had been against going into the lake from the outset but was still penalized for just being there. Lately Roger had also noticed that Krin-Tin was spending more time with Zinkie, and he feared that all of his friends were losing interest in him.

Although Roger was grateful that he was able to remain on Mon-Marg, he was very upset over what had happened in the lake. Sheriff Squarevicky had temporarily calmed his nerves, but Roger still had many unanswered questions. For instance, if it wasn't the missing key in the blue box, then what was in there? And if it was the key, what could be inside the volcano that was so important?

One evening after their punishment, Roger convinced Zinkie to come with him to see Gwan. An old tin sign that read Official Mon-Margian Personal Greeters' Headquarters was hanging above the door at the base of the mountain across from school. A cluster of leafy blue vines grew from the ground, covering the front of the building. Roger rang the buzzer, and within seconds a creature half his size with white and green stripes opened the door.

"May I help you?" it squeaked in a miniature voice.

"Yes, we're here to see Personal Greeter Gwan," said Roger.

"Come in then...come in." The creature hobbled aside to let the boys through.

Roger and Zinkie were led down a dark flight of stone stairs that brought them underground, down another corridor, and finally through a steel door with a sign that read: **TRAVEL AND TRANSPORTATION.**

The room was large—a hotbed of activity and noise. There were rows of desks, each containing a round computer screen. Most of the Personal Greeters were busy writing, typing, or watching movies about planets, galaxies, and solar systems. In the center of the room was a large pink globe that rotated slowly, displaying assignments.

The creature led Roger and Zinkie past the globe to the other side of the room, where Gwan sat at his desk watching a movie about planet Dubble-Zarg. His little furry feet were up on his desk, and his cane was propped up against the chair. When he saw Roger approaching, he threw down his feet and stood.

"Roger Webb! And how have you been?" He grabbed his top hat and put it on, covering his comical shock of white fur.

"Hey, Gwan," Roger said. "This is my friend, Zinkie Melou."

"Yes, yes, of course. Dr. Melou's son, I presume?" Gwan said dryly.

"Yes," Zinkie answered quickly. "I'm going to be head Space Director like him someday."

"Yes...well," Gwan said sarcastically. "Some of us obtain things much more easily than others."

"Well, Gwan, the reason I came to see you is because some very strange things have been going on, and I think something really bad might happen," Roger chattered nervously.

"What do you mean?" Gwan's round ears perked up, and a look of genuine concern crossed his face.

"Well," said Roger, reaching into his bag and handing the blue box to Gwan, "it all started with this. I found this box right before I came to Mon-Marg, and ever since I arrived here, I've been followed. The Muddshire Bogglings told me that the king is in danger, the noble sun is going to be destroyed by the evil star, and that someone had been trying to get into the ancient underwater gate." Roger paused and looked at the box. "I think this is the key to the gate, and I'm pretty sure it's the missing Gorr who's been following me because he knows I have it."

Gwan stared at Roger in disbelief. "Well," he finally said, exhaling dramatically. "I wasn't expecting all of this! Come here, you two, sit down." He pointed to some chairs near his desk. "First of all, what were you doing in Lake Fuddle Mudd? I told you to stay away from there!"

"I know...it was a dumb idea," said Roger, glaring at Zinkie. "We were caught by Sheriff Squarevicky and punished. I came here to ask if you knew anything else about the fifth Gorr, or if you might know what happened to that Personal Greeter who disappeared years ago. Anything at all to help me figure this out!"

Gwan sighed. "Well, I see that you've been very busy, Roger. And with the wrong things, I might add. I told you all I know about the missing Personal Greeter. He got an assignment just like those." He pointed to the big globe. "Then he went out to pick up the Inkytootian...but the two of them never returned. Their vector was found near the Fire Pits. And yes, the Gorrs were blamed." He lowered his eyes.

"Well, what if this holds the missing key?" asked Roger as he pointed to the blue box. "And what if Bowgee Berg hid this box for the Gorr to find in a Transport Bubble, and it fell out on Earth?" Gwan took the box, turned it over in his paws, and shook it.

"I don't think so," said Gwan.

"But it has to be something that the Gorr wants from me! Why else would he be stalking me?"

"I think some of your schoolmates might be playing a trick on you. If you wish, I'll take the box and find out what's in it. That way you won't have it in your possession, and you can relax." He studied the blue box closely, and Roger couldn't help but notice his eyes twinkling with curiosity.

"Okay," said Roger. He'd rather not have the box anyway. It had caused far too many problems already.

"I told him all that," Zinkie spoke up while casually flipping through a catalog of Gwan's Personal Greeter Ethics, visibly bored. "I think he's just being paranoid."

Roger sat thinking. He stared at the big globe in the center of the room as another assignment scrolled across the screen.

"Hey, Gwan," Roger said. "Where do those assignments come from? I mean...who gives them to the Personal Greeters?"

Gwan sighed, hesitated, then sighed again. "Well, I supposed it's too late to hide anything from you now...But you'll have to keep this quiet. This is top secret Travel and Transportation knowledge." They huddled closer.

"Up in the king's volcano, hidden away in the highest room, is his most important and valuable possession."

"What is it?" Zinkie and Roger's eyes widened.

"His pet," Gwan said.

"His pet?" asked Roger.

"The Glowing Rabbit," whispered Gwan. "The Glowing Rabbit was on this planet first. History tells us that many years before King Gloob discovered Mon-Marg, a giant meteoroid carrying the Glowing Rabbit crashed into the surface of the planet, creating the royal volcano. When the king discovered the planet years later, he found the rabbit living in the volcano...alone."

"What's so special about it?" Zinkie asked.

Gwan ignored his question and continued. "The king was kind to the rabbit, and the rabbit appreciated his kindness. As time went on, it shared its knowledge with the king, who soon found that the Glowing Rabbit knew the secrets to all space travel. It knew the coordinates and the directions to every single planet, star, and galaxy in the entire universe. The Space Directors don't even know how to get from one planet to the next. Only the Glowing Rabbit knows the directions. It sits in a gilded cage high in the volcano, printing out directions for the king, who programs all the Transport Bubbles and sends us these assignments." He pointed to the globe.

"Wow," said Roger and Zinkie at the same time.

"So, you see, that is why there is an invisible air shield around the volcano and why the Bogglings won't let anyone near the underwater gate. The king's assistant was the only other living soul to ever have access to the volcano and the Glowing Rabbit. But ever since he betrayed the king, the Glowing Rabbit works alone. That is why no one was allowed to see the face of the king's assistant before he was arrested—and why no one is allowed to see him as he sits in prison today. He knows too much, and the risk is too great."

Chapter Seventeen
THE KING'S FESTIVAL

R oger soon found that Mon-Margian winters were quite different from what he was used to. For 14 days straight, it snowed, covering the town from top to bottom. Everyone had to remain indoors, as it was difficult to tunnel through the heavy snow. Roger spent his winter break in isolation, mostly alone in his room, thinking of all that had happened and wondering if Gwan had found a way to open the blue box. Krin-Tin didn't have much interest in Roger's theories and had been spending most of his time on the Videophone with Zinkie, laughing and talking about TV shows. Roger was annoyed by Krin-Tin's sudden adoration of Zinkie and even thought he noticed a slight swagger in his walk lately.

By the time the last of the great snow had melted, Roger was more than ready to get outside, where the entire town of Zirgon was alive again. Plants and flowers were beginning to bloom, and the orange sun had finally reappeared, blazing in the clear green sky. The first group of Druttlechuck birds had migrated back for the spring, filling the air with their delicate cries of Ick-shaw...Ick-shaw.

The morning of the King's Festival finally arrived. Everyone in Zirgon, as well as Mon-Margians from surrounding towns, gathered in the center of town to see the king, who would venture from his volcano home and give his annual speech on the state of Mon-Marg. Roger and Krin-Tin heard the cheering and music all the way up from the middle of the mountain, where groups of excited Mon-Margians bustled down the paths. They met Zinkie and Glacindia at the fork in the road, and the four of them walked to the bottom and pushed through the crowds together.

Throughout the town, there was singing, dancing, and gaiety. Balloons and fireworks filled the spring air, which smelled of burnt sweets and buttery treats. Lining the streets were vendors in makeshift booths selling everything imaginable—food, souvenirs, toys, and novelty items.

The group stopped at a booth with a green A-Zargian woman holding a sign that read: **TALKING ROCKS—15 credits**. Roger thought they looked like plain old rocks. He picked one up, held it in the palm of his hand, and studied it closely.

"What do you mean, talking rocks?" he asked the vendor. Before the woman could answer him, two glassy eyes popped up from the rock and a gruff voice called out, "Hey, bub, watch it. I'm gettin' dizzy from all this movement!"

Startled, Roger almost dropped the rock. He stared at it as the others laughed and began picking through the other rocks in the pile.

"Well, don't drop me now, butterfingers," the rock said rudely, scowling at Roger.

"I–I'm sorry," Roger stammered.

"I–I'm sorry…," the little thing mocked Roger obnoxiously.

"Well, I…I just…," Roger began.

"Well, are ya just gonna stand there and stare at me all day, or are ya gonna give me a new home?" the rock said sarcastically, making a mopey face and blinking its eyes sadly.

"Well, I–I don't really think I can afford to…" Before Roger could finish the sentence, he felt a sharp pinch. The rock had bitten him!

"Ooouuch!" yelped Roger, tossing the rock back into the pile and clutching his hand in pain. The rock landed with a thud and a snide chuckle.

"See ya later, sucker!" the rock called from the pile and shut its eyes.

"Let's get out of here," said Roger to the others, a little flustered.

The group walked through the crowds towards the action in the center of town. Krin-Tin and Zinkie walked side by side, laughing and talking. Glacindia ran into her friend Pellia Frayzigar.

"Hey, guys! Wait up!" Roger shouted from behind, annoyed that no one was waiting for him.

"Oh, sorry," said Krin-Tin, as they slowed down.

"What were you guys laughing at?" asked Roger, catching up to them.

"Aww, nothing," said Zinkie. "Just something that happened on *The Milky Way Group*."

Just as he was going to ask what had happened, Roger felt something whiz by his face. Seconds later, it happened again.

"Hello!" a tiny voice called out. In front of the group, three flying creatures the size of Roger's hand appeared. Upon closer inspection, they looked exactly like kittens from Earth, with whiskers and tails, except that they had little wings on their backs that fluttered very fast, allowing them to hover. One kitten was orange, another was black and white, and the third one was pure white. They lingered in front of Roger, flicking their tails and mewing sweetly.

"I'm Meowquoli," said the black and white kitten. "And this is Noonie and Tip." The three kittens burst into little mewing laughter. "We're on our way to see the king!"

"Yes, so are we," said Roger, smiling at the tiny kittens.

Noonie, the orange kitten, landed on Roger's shoulder and began cleaning its paws.

"I'm just so filthy," squeaked Noonie, between licks. "I've been washing all day, and I just don't think I'm clean enough to see the king!"

"Well, I'm very tired," mewed Tip, curling up on Roger's other shoulder and letting out a big yawn. "I haven't gotten a wink of sleep in at least fifteen minutes!" And just like that, she was asleep, purring loudly. Roger eyed the two kittens and laughed. He looked at his friends, who were staring at the flying kittens in amazement.

"I'm soooo sorry about them," piped in Meowquoli. "They really have no manners at all." He flew down and started batting at a piece of thread hanging from Rogers jacket. He clawed and swatted, finally grasping it with his delicate paws. Roger watched it start to unravel.

"Hey!" cried out Zinkie suddenly. "That Spacemouse is trying to steal your card, Roger!"

Caught off guard, Roger looked down and saw a scrawny gray mouse with long whiskers and an orange vest trying to grab hold of the money card attached to Roger's belt.

"Hey!" yelled Roger, swatting the mouse away. It plopped to the ground and lay sprawled on its back.

"Well, s-o-o-o-o-r-r-r-y!" said the mouse lazily, drawing out the syllables. "A poor little Spacemouse can't get a break around here," he muttered, and scurried away, followed by the kittens.

"What just happened?" Roger asked.

"Those were Flying Gypsy Cats, Roger. They come to festivals and distract citizens while the Spacemouse tries to rob them. It's the oldest trick in the book!" Zinkie scoffed

"Well, then, why didn't you warn Roger when you saw them coming, Zinkie?" Glacindia asked accusingly.

"Because he needs to figure this stuff out on his own, that's why,

Glacindia. I mean...I had to learn everything the hard way, so why shouldn't he?" Zinkie began strutting away.

"If I'm not mistaken, Zinkie, didn't I hear that your father had to get your card and watch back at last year's festival? And didn't he teach you just about everything you've learned here on Mon-Marg?" asked Glacindia, hands on hips, ready for an argument. Roger blushed, happy that Glacindia was sticking up for him.

"No, he didn't!" said Zinkie defensively. "I've had to learn a lot on my own, you know, since my father is always out on important Space Director missions."

Roger knew he shouldn't say anything, but he was sick of Zinkie bragging about his father being such an important Mon-Margian. "Why do you always have to bring up the fact that your father is a Space Director, Zinkie? You always brag about him, just so you can make others feel bad." He didn't enjoy arguing, but he couldn't put up with Zinkie's obnoxious attitude any longer.

Zinkie's face flushed. He didn't like to be ganged up on. After a long pause, he responded with a vengeful sneer. "You know Roger, you're just jealous that my father is an important Mon-Margian. I mean, I can see why." Zinkie slowly raised his eyebrows. "Your father is just a common criminal who left you and doesn't care about you at all." He glared at Roger, his face now a deep shade of rusted metal, his mouth twitching at the corners.

Roger stared in shock at Zinkie, who glared back at him. He turned to Krin-Tin, who was staring at his boots. Roger couldn't believe Zinkie's words, which had struck him like a punch in the stomach. How could Krin-Tin have told Zinkie about his personal history? He had told Krin-Tin about his family in confidence! Roger felt salty tears welling up as he turned and pushed his way through

the noisy crowd.

"Roger!" Krin-Tin cried. "I'm sorry! I didn't mean to tell..."

"Roger!" He heard Glacindia call out. But he kept running through the packed streets of Zirgon. Finally she caught up with him.

"Roger!" she said, grabbing his arm. "You can't let Zinkie get to you! He only acts that way because his father is never around. He's really very lonely!" She stared at him pleadingly. But Roger was still upset. He couldn't believe Krin-Tin had betrayed his confidence, and he definitely didn't want Glacindia to see him cry.

"Just leave me alone, Glacindia!" he shouted, and ran away, leaving her in the middle of the jubilant crowd. He felt terrible and let down, just like he had always felt on Earth.

Chapter Eighteen

THE TRUTH ABOUT GORRS

The celebration continued as Roger made his way home. He could still see lights flashing and fireworks exploding as he ascended the deserted mountain path. Roger was alone, which was fine with him. He needed time to think.

Roger realized that Zinkie didn't mean to act that way. He just couldn't help it. His father was an important Space Director, and of course Zinkie wanted to brag about it. Roger was mainly upset with Krin-Tin, whom he had told about his family in confidence. Plus they had made a pact to go through the adventure together, and Roger had been feeling left out recently. His friends seemed to have pulled away, as if they thought he was weird or maybe dangerous.

A crackling sound in the bushes behind him interrupted his thoughts. He turned but saw only the empty path. Roger stood frozen, silent, and listening. Hearing nothing, he started walking again. But after hearing another crackling noise, Roger took off as fast as he could up the mountain, not daring to turn around.

Seconds later, he heard footsteps hitting the ground behind him. *The Gorr!* Blinded with fear, Roger ran faster than he ever had in his life. His legs felt like they were moving in quicksand, and his heavy backpack seemed to carry a ton of bricks. It was like a bad dream where he was stuck, running in place and getting nowhere. The footsteps behind him came closer and closer until suddenly something grabbed his shoulder.

But as Roger turned to face the evil Gorr, he instead saw Sheriff Squarevicky, the friendly Urggian, huffing and puffing to catch his breath.

"Roger! Roger! Relax...it'sss only me!" puffed the sheriff, easing his grip on Roger's shoulder.

"Sheriff Squarevicky!" Roger gasped, flustered but relieved. "You scared me!"

"Roger! I've been trying to find you all day!" panted the sheriff. "You have to come with me...you were right about the Gorr!" he stared at Roger, looking deeply distressed.

"What do you mean?"

"I wasss on my way to the King'sss Fessstival when I sssaw him! He was perched in the branchesss of a tree overlooking the main road into town. He wasss waiting for the king!"

"What did he look like?" Roger asked, his voice shaking.

"Oh, he looked more evil than even I remembered, Roger! I've never sssseen anything more hideousss. His eyesss were chilling amber sssslitsss, hisss teeth were long and sharp, and his sssskin wasss white and sssscaly! He wasss frothing at the mouth, and green ssslime oozed from his poresss."

"What happened then?" Roger responded anxiously.

"Well, asss I looked up at him, waiting in that tree, he sssaw me! He glared at me hatefully and exposssed hisss razor sharp teeth and long yellow clawsss. Then with a look of defianssse, he held up a key, before jumping out of the tree and darting towardsss town. I know that he isss going there to kill the king, and then to the volcano to get the Glowing Rabbit! He'sss going to program the Transsssport Bubblesss back to Gorrinth sssso he can bring back more of the Gorrsss. We can't let that happen!"

"Wh-what do you need me for?" asked Roger.

"I need you to come with me and tell the king exactly what the

Muddshire Bogglingsss told you. Alssso, from what you've told me, I don't think you're sssafe either! Come on, let'sss go!" he said urgently.

The sheriff grabbed Roger's arm, and they ran back down the path. Roger's mind was racing. He knew that he'd been followed and that the Gorr was determined to overthrow the king and rule Mon-Marg. Finally someone else believed him! He just hoped it wasn't too late.

They reached the bottom of the mountain where the Patrolvector was waiting, and sped off towards town. The trees and empty road soon gave way to the edge of town and the crowded streets of Zirgon. The festival was still in full swing. Roger peered into every alleyway and side street expecting to see the Gorr squatting in the shadows. His heart was pounding and his stomach churned with fear. Would they get there in time? He glanced at Sheriff Squarevicky, who was looking nervously in the rearview mirror to make certain they weren't being followed.

Roger suddenly froze. A chill started at the base of his spine, and slowly crept up until he felt goose bumps all over.

I must be seeing things.

He turned back towards Sheriff Squarevicky, who was still looking nervously in the mirror. Roger heard Zinkie's voice echoing in his head.

All Urggians are allergic to their own reflection. If they catch even the slightest glimpse of themselves, they freeze up and die.

Roger felt his knees start to shake.

"What'sss the matter, Roger?"

"Y-you're not really from planet Urg, are you?" asked Roger slowly.

The sheriff's eyes narrowed ever so slightly, and his lips curled into a sly grin. "So, you've figured out my little secret," he said quietly and gazed at Roger with vacant black eyes. His voice had changed completely—it was low and raspy. "Well, I guess I can take these uncomfortable things off then," he growled, pulling off his gloves to reveal bony fingers with long yellow claws. His hands were gray and spotted, with tufts of ratty fur

"W–what…w–who are you then?" stammered Roger, sliding as far away from the sheriff as he could.

"What I am," said the sheriff casually. "Is an Inkytootian. Who I am is the future ruler of Mon-Marg." He let out a long, loud cackle that bounced off the walls of the vehicle and rang in Roger's ears. His snake tongue shot out grotesquely. "With your help, of course…." he added menacingly.

The Inkytootian parked in front of the Police Station on the far edge of Zirgon. The area was deserted because everyone was in the center of town, celebrating with the king. The sheriff pulled Roger from the vehicle and into the station, hissing, "There's no one around to rescue you, Roger."

"But…I can't help you get into the volcano! I don't have the key! Why are you taking me here?" he yelled desperately as the sheriff dragged him roughly down a long corridor. They stood at the top of the stairs while the sheriff fidgeted with his keys. He unlocked a door and dragged Roger down a dark, musty stairwell. Cobwebs lined the walls, filthy water dripped from the ceiling, and small creatures were scurrying around. At the bottom of the stairs they proceeded down another dingy hallway to a large cage with bars that had been built into the wall. Roger could make out the shape of a creature huddled in the corner covered by a black blanket.

Roger's heart was pounding. His knees shook as the Inkytootian raked his claws against the cage, making a terrible screeching sound.

"Wake up! You have a visitor. It's someone that you will be thrilled to see," taunted the sheriff.

Roger had to steady himself against the wall as the blanket slowly began to move. He closed his eyes, not wishing to see what was curled up in the corner of that wretched cell. The deafening silence was broken by a soft, deep voice.

"Roger?"

Roger slowly opened his eyes and gasped. It couldn't be. His eyes had to be playing tricks on him. He gripped the bars of the cell in order to keep from falling. His head began to spin, and he felt himself losing his balance. The last thing he heard before passing out was the muffled sound of his own voice.

"Dad?"

Chapter Nineteen

A MIRACLE

Roger opened his eyes slowly and watched a Crawling Wendel scurry across the ceiling. He was shivering, and the steady sound of dripping water echoed throughout the dungeon. He looked at the man in the cell. There was no mistaking it—the man under the blanket was George Webb, Roger's father. His face was much thinner than Roger remembered, and his hair and beard were long from years of neglect, but Roger knew it was him as soon as he saw his eyes. They were the same green eyes that had danced in the moonlight years ago, while he had pointed up at the stars.

"Roger! Are you all right?" His father's voice was full of urgency.

"Yes, Dad! I-I can't believe you're here!" Roger was shocked and confused.

The Inkytootian sheriff interrupted them with a long howling cackle. "I'm soooo glad the two of you are having a nice reunion. But, if you don't mind, Mr. George Webb...or should I say...Bowgee Berg? Ha ha, how clever—he rearranged the letters of his name." He nudged Roger hard in the ribs. "I need to get on with my extraordinary plan of ruling the universe. So if you will be so kind as to tell me the location of the key?" He clutched Roger roughly by the arm, pinching the skin and nearly drawing blood.

Roger couldn't believe that all this time, he had thought it was the fifth Gorr who was after the key. But it had actually been the Inkytootian! The Inkytootian needed Roger in order to blackmail his father, the king's assistant, so he would disclose the location of the key!

The situation seemed dire, and Roger knew he had to do something quick. "Wait!" he said, stalling for time. He loosened himself from the sheriff's grip and took off his backpack. "I think I may have what you need." Rummaging through his backpack, he tried to think of something—anything—that would distract the sheriff and buy some time. As he struggled to come up with an excuse, he came across the little plastic crocodile that his father had given him so many years ago. He pulled out the toy and held it up for his father to see.

"Remember this, Dad?"

His father's eyes widened, and Roger thought he noticed him shake his head ever so slightly.

The Inkytootian ripped the plastic crocodile out of Roger's hands, his eyes ablaze. "Enough of the nostalgia! What do you have in there for me!?" he demanded. His face contorted into a vicious grimace, and he hurled the toy at the wall with all his strength.

Roger winced as the little crocodile smashed into the wall, cracking into a hundred pieces and clattering to the ground in a broken heap. Among the cacophony of plastic, one piece in particular made a unique sound as it skidded across the stone floor— *Clink...clink...clangedy....ping.* Astonished, Roger stared at what had fallen out of the toy. Lying amongst the shards of plastic was a golden key encrusted with exquisite, sparkling diamonds.

"Ha!" cried the sheriff, diving to reach the priceless key. "I didn't realize how very easy this would be!" He grinned wickedly. "I thought you would have picked a more creative place to hide this, Berg. However, this will do." Before Roger could react, the sheriff turned, dashed down the hallway and up the stairs, howling with laughter.

"Dad!" Roger cried. "What's going on? What are we going to do? He's going to the volcano! No one will be able to stop him because

they're all at the King's Festival!"

"Come here, son." His father reached through the bars, giving him a big hug. Roger started to cry. His tears were a mixture of joy, sadness, and fear.

"How did you end up here, Dad?" Roger asked, his voice shaking.

"Roger, there is so much I have to explain to you, but there is no time now. You must stop the Inkytootian!" his father said.

"But how are we going to save Mon-Marg?" he asked.

"First you have to go upstairs into Sheriff Squarevicky's office and find a Flabbergaster."

"A Flabbergaster?" Roger asked incredulously. "What's a Flabbergaster?"

"The police have small devices called Flabbergasters that are used to stop creatures who get out of control. All you have to do is aim it at the sheriff, push the red button, and he'll freeze for five minutes. Just keep repeating the procedure until help arrives. But you must be careful!" he urged. "Don't let the Inkytootian get hold of the device and use it on you! You have no idea what evil he is capable of!"

"I'll be careful, Dad. I'll stop the sheriff, then I'll come back and find a way to get you out of here!" Roger ran up the stairs to the main office and found the Flabbergaster that his father had described—a small black box with wires on the front. He placed it in his bag.

As Roger raced down the hall, the mysterious words of the Muddshire Bogglings suddenly made sense. All along he had thought that the Bogglings had been telling him that the noble sun was in danger. A chill came over him as he realized that he, Roger, was the noble son who was in danger—and the evil star the Bogglings had referred to was none other than the badge-wearing sheriff.

Chapter Twenty

PURSUIT

O nce outside, Roger saw that the sheriff's Patrolvector was gone, which meant that he was headed for the volcano. Roger could still hear the celebration from the King's Festival. As he ran towards Lake Fuddle Mudd, he thought about getting help from some of the townsfolk but realized that there wasn't enough time.

After all those years of believing that George Webb had abandoned his family, Roger still couldn't believe that his father was right here on Mon-Marg. *Wait until Zinkie hears that my father, George Webb, was once the king's assistant, the most important creature on all of Mon-Marg aside from the king!*

Rounding the path, Roger saw the bubbling green lake shimmering in the sunlight. On the far shore, the magnificent volcano rose from the water, its rocky peak breaking through the swirling clouds.

Roger was planning on diving into the lake and then holding his breath in hopes of catching a quick ride to the gate from a helpful Boggling. But as he got ready to jump in, he felt something cold and clammy on his shoulder. He was spun around forcefully and found himself looking straight into the eyes of the Inkytootian.

"I see you've followed me, just as I suspected you would," the sheriff growled in his raspy voice. "Just like your father...don't know to quit when you're ahead!" Squeezing Roger's shoulder, his claws punctured the skin, causing blood to run slowly down Roger's arm.

"Please, just let me go!" begged Roger.

"I couldn't have asked for a better ending. Now the only decision I have to make is how to dispose of you. Hmmm...shall it be the Fire Pits, just like that Personal Greeter? Or the Spitting Cactus Trees, like that pesky Sheriff Jijijian? Or perhaps I can take you down to the Flintosaurus cage. I hear they're very hungry at this time of year."

"Please!" Roger pleaded.

The Inkytootian took a long piece of rope from his utility belt. He pushed Roger to the ground and began wrapping the rope around his hands. Then he secured it tightly around his legs with a large knot. When he was finished, Roger couldn't move. He just lay on the ground, staring up at the tall, menacing lizard.

"W–what are you going to do now?"

The reptile gave a low, rumbling growl, and his face twisted into an evil sneer. He bent down and...*click*...unhooked Roger's Language Decoder. Then as Roger watched helplessly...*click*...he unhooked his Atmos-Pack as well. Roger looked up in a stupor as the Inkytootian let out another long howling cackle and disappeared into the lake with a splash.

Roger began screaming at the top of his lungs in hopes that someone would hear him. He couldn't take his eyes off of the dangling wire connected to his Atmos-Pack. Dr. Von Tibbetson had warned him that once the wire was unhooked, there would be a ten-minute reserve supply. After that had run out, he would float away into outer space.

Roger felt the thick rope with his fingers and tried to maneuver his hands free, but it was useless. The rope was too tight. He didn't know how many minutes had passed, but his breathing had already become labored, and his shoulder throbbed. He tried calling out, but his voice was soft and weak. He laid his head on the ground. *This is it. This is how I will die—alone on a strange planet, away*

from my family and friends. He pictured himself drifting aimlessly through the vast universe forever. He used to imagine all of the possibilities that the great sky held and would dream about life on other planets. Never in his worst nightmare did he imagine any of this.

Soon Roger found it extremely difficult to breathe, and his body started to feel weightless. It was happening. He started to rise ever so slowly. He tried to reach down with his fingers, but he was too weak. Before long he was hovering at least two feet above the ground, and he felt completely numb.

When Roger had risen three feet, he began to see stars. Somewhere in his head, he heard faint noises.

"Gurdunk-shay! Gurdunk-shay!" He slowly tilted his head to the right and made out three blurry shapes. Roger felt something grab and tug at him.

"Bligmay shak, uz, wee beezonfrow!!"

"Styz Par Fasdix Roo Wan Hette!!"

"Kully Kully, Zip Zan Zeedle Zee?"

Then there was blackness.

Chapter Twenty-One

THAT'S WHAT FRIENDS ARE FOR

oger opened his eyes. Taking a deep breath, he saw Krin-Tin, Zinkie, and Glacindia staring down at him and realized he'd been untied and his Language Decoder and Atmos-Pack had been reconnected. "Roger!" shouted Krin-Tin. "You're okay! We looked everywhere for you!"

"Poor Roger! What happened?" cried Glacindia, tears in her eyes. "Why were you tied up?"

"Your Atmos-Pack and Language Decoder were unhooked! We thought you were dead!" Zinkie chimed in.

"How long have I been out?" Roger sat up, feeling dazed.

"Not very long after we plugged you back in. Oh, I'm soooo glad you're all right!" Glacindia hugged Roger, while Krin-Tin hick-honked thankfully.

But Roger's bewilderment turned to panic as he remembered the Inkytootian and the Glowing Rabbit. "I have so much to tell you guys, but there's no time now. I have to go into Lake Fuddle Mudd!" Roger got up abruptly, making sure the Flabbergaster was still tucked away inside his backpack.

"Are you crazy?" yelled Glacindia. "After what you just went through? Look at you...you're bleeding!! Who did this to you!"

"Yeah, we felt awful about what happened at the festival," said Zinkie apologetically, shuffling his big gold feet.

"There's no time now! Go into town and get someone to warn the king that the planet is in danger. Sheriff Squarevicky is the missing Inkytootian, and he's the one who committed all of the crimes—not the Gorrs. He's on his way to the Glowing Rabbit right now! He has the missing key to the volcano gate and is going to take over Mon-Marg! I have to stop him!" Before anyone could argue, he took off towards the lake.

"Wait!" a voice cried out.

Roger turned and saw Krin-Tin running clumsily towards him in his oversized boots.

"You're not going alone!" Krin-Tin caught up with Roger, huffing and puffing.

"What... you're coming with me?" Roger was dumbfounded. He couldn't believe that Krin-Tin, who was afraid of his own shadow, would actually follow him on such a dangerous mission. "But what about your allergies?"

Krin-Tin shrugged his bony shoulders. "That's what friends are for, I guess," he smiled. "We're in this together...remember?"

Roger smiled.

"I never meant to tell Zinkie about your family. We were just talking and...you know how persuasive he can be."

"It's okay," Roger said. "Really. Now are you ready?"

Krin-Tin nodded nervously. "Ready."

The two of them took a deep breath and jumped into the bubbling lake. Just as Roger had hoped, the head Muddshire Boggling was waiting for them. The Boggling seemed hysterical as she dragged Roger and Krin-Tin towards the underwater city.

"Hurry, hurry, danger's here,
It's getting very late!
We've not much time before he reaches
The forbidden gate."

Roger nodded, dizzy from holding his breath. He saw the lights lining the path to the city, and soon the three of them were passing the curious sea creatures, who watched from their shell houses in wide-eyed anticipation. Roger felt a huge responsibility—the future of the planet was now in his hands.

The Boggling dropped them off directly in front of the unlocked entrance at the base of the volcano, and Roger pushed open the heavy iron gate. Magically it swung shut behind them without allowing any water inside. Roger quickly exhaled and stood for a moment to catch his breath.

"Are you all right, Krin-Tin?" Roger wheezed.

"I'm fine." Krin-Tin sputtered and coughed, slapping his pointed ears to unclog them.

They were finally inside the great volcano. Roger and Krin-Tin stood on the end of a creaky wooden plank that stretched across to the other side, held up by thick ropes. Below them was a fiery pool of bubbling lava. The sizzling flames shot up, threatening to consume anything they touched.

The conical mass had rocky stairwells that ascended the steep, craggy walls and wound upward towards a large platform. The platform resembled a bridge that jutted out from the wall. It was held firmly by two heavy golden chains. Roger could see the rabbit's blue glow coming from somewhere near the center of the platform. Among the numerous stairwells and landings, dark caves dotted the walls—living areas for the king and his family.

"A-chooonk!" Krin-Tin sneezed. "I think the dampness is making me sick," he said miserably.

"Just a little while longer, Krin-Tin. We're almost there," Roger reassured him.

They inched cautiously to the other side of the bridge and followed the Inkytootian's wet footprints up the winding maze of stairs and past the cavelike rooms and muddy catacombs. Roger could tell they were nearing the top. The blue glow was stronger, and the foreboding pool of fire was much farther below them. Emerging from a covered stairwell, they finally reached the door, which opened out onto the platform.

"Wow," whispered Krin-Tin.

The platform was much like the one down below, but wider and sturdier—secured to the walls by massive golden chains. The boys were closer to the open mouth of the volcano now. They could see the cool green sky above and the menacing pool of lava below.

Sitting on the platform in a beautiful golden cage was a rabbit, no bigger or smaller than any rabbit Roger had ever seen. It had long ears, buck teeth, and a puffy tail. Although it looked like an ordinary rabbit, there was nothing ordinary about the hypnotizing blue glow that filled the room and made Roger feel calm. The Inkytootian had rested the key to the volcano on top of the cage.

"The Glowing Rabbit," whispered Roger.

"What are we going to do, Roger?" sniffed Krin-Tin.

Standing over the rabbit, his scaly back towards the entrance, was the Inkytootian. He was reading something underneath the cage. Looking closer, Roger saw that it was a computer screen with numbers, codes, and names on it. The computer recorded the rabbit's thoughts! Near the edge of the platform was the machine used to program the Transport Bubbles. In order to send them out, all the Inkytootian needed to do was to type in coordinates and directions to any planet. Roger heard the sheriff growl to the Glowing Rabbit, "Now give me directions to Inkytootia."

The rabbit twitched its nose, and the coordinates popped up on the computer screen. Roger realized that they had to act fast. The sheriff was getting the directions to Inkytootia, so he could send ships to pick up evil creatures just like him who would conquer Mon-Marg!

Keeping an eye on the Inkytootian, Roger quietly reached around and got the Flabbergaster out of his bag,

"What are you going to do?" Krin-Tin mouthed to Roger.

"Shhh. Just stay here!"

The very sight of the wicked Inkytootian made Roger shudder. He could hear the sheriff growling softly to himself as he waited for the Glowing Rabbit to print out the coordinates and directions to Inkytootia. Roger knew he had to act immediately. Once the Transport Bubbles were programmed and sent on their way, there could be no reversing their course.

Roger took a deep breath and crept through the entrance. His eyes never left the Inkytootian, who was hunched over the programming machine. Roger moved past the Glowing Rabbit to the center of the room and stopped directly behind the sheriff. Raising the Flabbergaster, he was ready to press the button, when all of a sudden...

"A-chooonk!" Krin-Tin's sneeze echoed off the cavernous walls.

The Inkytootian swung around, startling Roger, who pressed the button a moment too late. The sheriff's long arm swung violently, knocking the Flabbergaster from Roger's trembling hands. It clattered to the ground, slid to the far corner of the platform, and stopped just at the edge.

"Run, Krin-Tin! Run!" Roger yelled. Krin-Tin bounded down the steps, leaving Roger alone with the Inkytootian.

"So," the creature said, gripping Roger by the neck. "You didn't learn from your first mistake, did you?" He flashed his long fangs and dug his claws further into Roger's neck. Roger kicked and punched desperately as he was dragged over to where the Flabbergaster was balanced.

"Didn't you learn not to snoop through grown-up things?" the Inkytootian hissed as he picked up the device. "Curious about my toys, are you? Well, maybe you'd like to see how it works—how it feels to be shocked?" He pointed the Flabbergaster directly at Roger's face. With one final burst of energy, Roger twisted out of the Inkytootian's grip and ducked just in time to avoid the immobilizing spark.

But the look on the Inkytootian's face told Roger that something was terribly wrong.

The Flabbergaster's electrical current had missed Roger completely and instead had shot directly into the path of the Glowing Rabbit. The rabbit was frozen solid. The sheriff dropped the Flabbergaster in shock, and it bounced to the other end of the platform.

Before either one of them could react, the temperature inside the volcano increased drastically. Down below the lava bubbled fiercely. Smoke and ash billowed towards the opening. Was the volcano going to erupt? The rabbit's blue glow began to dull—first to a dark blue, then purple, and suddenly a deep, dark red. Roger coughed and sputtered from the thick smoke. The computer screens flashed, and the codes became strange symbols. The crazed sheriff seemed to have completely forgotten that Roger was in the room. He started banging on the cage, pressing buttons wildly.

Roger knew he had to do something quickly. The Inkytootian was only making things worse by toying with the controls, and he was surely going to kill Roger as soon as he remembered him. With one lucky grab, Roger yanked the Atmos-Pack from the sheriff's belt and ran to the other side of the platform.

The sheriff turned to Roger with a look of pure evil. His eyes were black slits, and he bared his sharp fangs, hissing and growling. "You give that back...do you hear me?" He moved closer.

"Stay back or I'll drop it!" cried Roger, holding the Atmos-Pack over the edge of the platform.

"No!" the Inkytootian shouted, and he lunged at Roger.

Roger knew what he needed to do. Even though it would most likely be the end of him, he had no choice. Uncurling his fingers, he let the Atmos-Pack fall into the lava below. At the exact same moment from across the room, sizzling shock filled the air.

Roger, waiting for the Inkytootian to take him over the edge, suddenly realized that the sheriff was frozen inches away in mid-lunge, a look of surprise on his face.

"Krin-Tin!" Roger yelled. There was Krin-Tin, in the doorway, holding the Flabbergaster. He looked frazzled and sick, but he had saved Roger's life.

"I wasn't going to leave you alone up here!" sniffled Krin-Tin, running towards Roger. As he helped Roger up, the Glowing Rabbit began to twitch. The room cooled, the smoke filtered out, and the angry red glow returned to a cool blue. Roger and Krin-Tin stared in silence at the frozen Inkytootian.

Roger and Krin-Tin kept the evil creature frozen for ten more minutes, and soon the Inkytootian suffered the consequences of not having an Atmos-Pack. At first the changes were gradual, and he began slowly lifting into the air. Roger watched him rise up and up until he floated from the open mouth of the volcano at around the same time the effect of the Flabbergaster wore off. The sheriff looked

down helplessly, writhing and spitting in anger.

"Someday I'll get you for this, Roger Webb!" The Inkytootian rose higher and higher into the air like a child's lost balloon—past the swirling clouds, past the changing moon, until he was just a speck in the early evening sky. Roger smiled at Krin-Tin and breathed a deep sigh of relief.

Upon his triumphant return from the volcano, Roger reunited with his father, who explained everything to him. George Webb described how he had been chosen for The Space Program many years ago, just as Roger had been chosen. He spent his time between Mon-Marg, where he befriended the king, and Earth, where he met Beatrice and started a family. He spoke of the king's offer to become his assistant and of the complete trust that was offered to him.

"Not long after that, five Gorrs came to Mon-Marg to be in The Space Program," his father told him. "They started off as very nice creatures, but they soon became a problem. When I heard about the missing Inkytootian and the Personal Greeter, and then the death of Sheriff Jijijian, I too made the mistake of assuming it was the Gorrs who were to blame. But now I know that they were just mischievous—they weren't killers. When Squarevicky offered to step up and become the new sheriff, I made the worst mistake of all. I met with him face-to-face to discuss the problem. Once he saw my true identity, he was able to frame me. I should have known that Squarevicky was the missing Inkytootian! But he physically resembled the Urgs to such an extent that I never even thought to look at his hands."

"Why did the king believe the sheriff instead of you, Dad?" asked Roger.

"Well, I realized that something wasn't right when after Squarevicky and I rounded up the five Gorrs—yes, all five of them—he told everyone that one was still missing. I should have gone straight to the king and told him about the sheriff's lie. Instead I came down to Earth and hid the key in your crocodile. I knew Squarevicky was up to something. I planned to get to the bottom of his lie, and then retrieve the key when I felt it was all cleared up," his father explained. "That was the last time I saw you or your mother."

"I remember that night!" Roger said. "It was the night you and Mom had that argument, and I watched your car disappear down the street."

His father paused. "Your mother didn't want me to go back." He looked at Roger sadly. "She knew something was wrong up here. She was upset that I was going and feared that something terrible might happen to me."

"You mean...she knew?" Roger was stunned. He had a flashback of the day his mother dropped the flowers on the floor after he had shown her what he had found in the forest. He had thought she said, "Those darn Martians are everywhere!" He knew now that she must have said, "Those Mon-Margians are everywhere!"

"Yes...she knew, Roger. She knew all about The Space Program. We were going to wait until you were old enough to tell you about Mon-Marg. We even had plans to move here permanently," his father explained.

Roger couldn't believe that his mother had known all along about The Space Program. The whole story of Newton's Academy of Scientific Children and the Loggerhead Sea Turtles was pointless. She had known exactly where Roger was going!

"You have to realize, Roger, that your mother would never have allowed you to come if she had known how dangerous things were up here."

"I think she knew that I'd find you," Roger said, remembering his mother's words. *I think you'll find everything you've been looking for.*

"Maybe she did," his father said pensively.

"So what happened after you left?" Roger asked.

"Well, by the time I returned to Mon-Marg, Squarevicky had already gotten to the king. He told him I had been secretly plotting with the fifth Gorr to take over the planet. Then King Gloob demanded that I return the key. I refused to tell him where I'd hidden it because I didn't want to put you or your mother in danger. The sheriff locked me up and told everyone that I had hidden the key somewhere in town...he thought that I had. The king lost all trust in me and hasn't wanted to see or speak to me since."

"But I don't understand. The FBI came to our house and everything! They said you stole money from your company!" said Roger.

"Those were members of The Space Program. They were probably instructed to search the house for the key. That must have been how they found out I had a son." He shook his head regretfully. "I never wanted you to be involved in any of this, Roger."

'So that's why I was chosen in the lottery!" exclaimed Roger. "The sheriff is on the Space Committee! It wasn't luck or destiny that I was chosen. He fixed the whole thing! He wanted to blackmail you with my life!"

"Exactly," said Mr. Webb. "He had to wait until you turned ten to get you into The Space Program."

□ □ □ □ □ □ □ □ □ □ □

The key to the volcano gate was returned to the king, and George Webb was released from prison. He told the king how the Inkytootian had killed the Personal Greeter, and then Sheriff Jijijian. Finally he explained how the Inkytootian had framed him when he had returned to Mon-Marg after hiding the key. The king regained his trust in his dearest friend and joyously reinstated him as his personal assistant. Roger's father had told King Gloob that he was honored but expressed his wish to first return to Earth to spend some time with his wife, Beatrice.

Later that week, a celebration was held in honor of Roger and Krin-Tin. The citizens of Zirgon were clamoring to see the heroes who had saved Mon-Marg from the evil Inkytootian. Roger sat between his father and Krin-Tin in the middle of the stage and looked out over the huge crowd. Also on stage were King Gloob and his family—the queen and two sons. Shortly after the volcano incident, Roger had found that communicating with the king was unlike anything he had ever experienced. Although the king didn't speak, Roger could understand exactly what the king was thinking. The king had asked questions about the events that had taken place through his mind, and Roger had answered out loud.

The night glittered with fireflies, the air was warm and breezy, and the blue moon cast a beautiful light over the town. In the front row were Zinkie Melou and Glacindia Garlian, along with other classmates and friends—including the beaming Dr. Von Tibbetson and the proud Schleffinschlubbs. Even Zinkie's father was there, and Zinkie couldn't have looked happier or prouder sitting next to him.

As for Roger, he was thrilled to be reunited with his father and happy with the thought of returning to Earth and surprising his mother. He would miss the wonderful friends he had made during the school year but looked forward to joining them next year for the sixth sector.

"Do you believe all of this is for us?" Krin-Tin nudged Roger excitedly.

As he sat waving to the grateful crowd, Roger noticed a small figure pushing its way towards the front of the stage. As it got closer, he realized that it was little Gwan, wildly waving something in the air.

"Roger! Roger!" he panted.

It was the mysterious blue box. Roger had almost forgotten about it after all that had happened. Before Gwan could say anything else, Dr. Von Tibbetson yelled across the crowd to Gwan.

"Why...you...little thief! My teeth! You thtole my teeth! I've been looking for thosth for tho long!" He grabbed the box out of Gwan's paw and dug into his pocket for a key. He took a set of false teeth from the box, and popped them into his mouth.

"There, that's much, much better. Now I sound simply superb!" He smiled at Roger, revealing a set of sparkling straight teeth.

"All that trouble over a set of false teeth," Roger said to Krin-Tin, shaking his head.

"I told you that it was nothing," Zinkie piped up from below.

"Shut up, Zinkie!" Glacindia punched Zinkie in the arm and smiled up at Roger.

Roger looked out at the sea of alien faces that had once seemed strange but now appeared friendly—and quite "normal." He looked past the fireflies dancing in the night, up towards the sky with its millions of twinkling stars, and he tried to imagine which light was Earth. His father smiled and pointed to a star way off to the left. It was flickering and bright and seemed to be signaling Roger home.